J. R. R. TOLKIEN
FOR BEGINNERS®

J. R. R. TOLKIEN

F O R   B E G I N N E R S ®

BY LOUIS MARKOS
ILLUSTRATED BY JEFF FALLOW

FOR BEGINNERS®

For Beginners LLC
30 Main Street, Suite 303
Danbury, CT 06810 USA
www.forbeginnersbooks.com

A For Beginners® Documentary Comic Book
Copyright © 2022

Cataloging-in-Publication information is available from the Library of Congress.

ISBN # 978-1-939994-82-0 Trade

Manufactured in the United States of America

Typography by Dana Hayward

For Beginners® and Beginners Documentary Comic Books® are published by For Beginners LLC.

First Edition

10 9 8 7 6 5 4 3 2 1

This book is dedicated to

Two Lewis-Tolkien scholars and
Three professor/role models

Who played the role of Gandalf for
My son Alex and daughter Anastasia

Holly Ordway & Michael Ward
Barbara Elliott, Rhonda Furr & David Kirkwood

Contents

J. R. R. TOLKIEN
FOR BEGINNERS®

Introduction

AS THE SECOND MILLENNIUM drew to a close, several polls of the British and American reading public were taken to determine the best book of the century. To the dismay of academics and literary critics on both sides of the Atlantic, *The Lord of the Rings* was consistently awarded the number one spot on the list.

Free from gritty language, graphic violence, and gratuitous sex, *The Lord of the Rings* is also, perhaps more surprisingly, free from skepticism and cynicism, Nietzschean nihilism and existential despair, Freudian psychoanalysis and Marxist ideology, feminist resentment and Darwinian naturalism. How then could it be chosen as the best book of the twentieth century, that beleaguered, war-torn century that gave us the culture of narcissism, the sexual revolution, endless political scandals, the hermeneutics of suspicion, postmodern deconstruction, and the fifteen minutes of fame?

Can there be any novel further from the culture and ethos of the twentieth century, any novel more decidedly pre-modern in scope? I have often noticed that a large percentage of the people who attend Renaissance festivals in full medieval garb would disagree with the social, political, economic, spiritual, sexual, and marital beliefs of the Middle Ages. In the same way, a large percentage of Tolkien fans have little sympathy for Tolkien's medieval worldview. And yet, they return again and again to Middle-earth. Why?

The reason, I believe, is that *The Lord of the Rings* taps a deep root in the human psyche. There is much death and destruction and defeat in Tolkien's world, but there is even more friendship and courage and hope. What one remembers when one finishes reading *The Lord of the*

Rings is not the vice of the villains, as strong and as well drawn as it is, but the virtue that empowers the heroes to resist it, even at the cost of their own lives.

Moderns are attracted to Middle-earth for many of the same reasons they are attracted to the original Star Wars trilogy: because both play on archetypal characters and patterns that have resonance in all times and cultures. The orphaned foundling who is called upon to be the unlikely hero (Frodo, Luke Skywalker), the wise old man who instructs the young hero (Gandalf, Obi-Wan Kenobi), the villain who was once good but was tempted to the dark side by power and forbidden knowledge (Saruman, Darth Vader), the greater, irredeemable villain behind the villain (Sauron, the Evil Emperor), the lone survivor who learns self-sacrifice and marries the princess (Aragorn and Arwen, Han Solo and Princess Leia).

All these and more play their roles in the grand narrative that Tolkien and George Lucas wove out of the strands of a thousand previous tales. All the heroes participate in their own personal quests, pilgrimages, and rites of passage, while also working together to ensure the triumph of good over evil, light over darkness, loyalty over treachery. The villains, meanwhile, seek ever to disrupt and twist and pervert the lands and peoples and customs of Middle-earth.

Like Lucas, Tolkien sweeps us away to a distant time and place that is also our own time and place, a world where difficult choices must be made and are made, where character is defined by those choices, and where redemption is possible though not always embraced.

But Tolkien does more, gives us

what the entire Star Wars franchise of films and novels never quite does: a fully lived-in world made up of numerous, often warring, races of angelic Valar and Maiar, Elves and Dwarves, Men and Hobbits who speak their own unique languages, have their own unique interactions with the earth, possess their own unique cultures, and tell their own unique stories of the good life and of what must be sacrificed to pre-serve it.[1]

He also includes a transcendent spiritual dimension of good-ness, truth, and beauty, and an affirmation of the four classical and three Christian virtues (courage, self-control, wisdom, and justice; faith, hope, and love) that add greater, metaphysical meaning and pur-pose to the choices made and the consequences that fol-low in their wake.

The things and the peoples and the struggles of Middle-earth seem more real and more vital than those of our world; the joys and the sorrows, the camaraderie and the division, the victories and the losses are richer, weightier, more fully realized.

How did Tolkien accomplish this? By so reinvigorating and reworking the epics of Homer and Virgil, Dante and Milton, Beowulf and the Volsunga

---

[1] In keeping with Tolkien's own practice, I will, throughout this book, capitalize species names for Men, Elves, Dwarves, Hobbits, etc. Only when I am speaking about specific men or elves or Dwarves or Hobbits will I use lowercase. I will also follow Tolkien's lead in cap-italizing the Ring and the Road.

saga—not to mention Genesis and Exodus—as to create a new genre: epic fantasy. While writing in prose rather than poetry and while crafting a new myth rather than passing down an old one, Tolkien's epic fantasy nevertheless deals in the same timeless, centrally human issues of life and death, mortality and immortality, permanence and change, duty and tyranny, love and betrayal, the longing for home and the inability to return home, the fulfillment of the destiny for which one was born and the loss of one's core identity and intrinsic worth.

It will be the goal of this book to introduce the reader to the multilayered depth and breadth of Tolkien's tales of Middle-earth, what critics, following Tolkien's lead, refer to collectively as his legendarium. To do justice to the full dimensions of that legendarium, I will speak in two voices: that of the storyteller who loves the stories he tells and that of the critic who seeks to identify and explicate key themes from those stories. In my telling and my analysis, I will treat the legendarium both as a collection of secondary-world myths with their own integrity and as a reflection of Tolkien's Catholic worldview.

This dual approach will allow me to remain faithful to what Tolkien himself explained to Father Robert Murray in a letter dated December 2, 1953, about eight months before *The Fellowship of the Ring* appeared in print: "*The Lord of the Rings* is of course a fundamentally religious and Catholic work; unconsciously so at first, but consciously in the revision. That is why I have not put in, or have cut out, practically all references to anything like 'religion,' to cults or practices, in the imaginary world. For the religious element is absorbed into the story and the symbolism."

As for organization, it must be understood that the order in which Tolkien wrote often differs greatly from the order in which what he wrote was published. As such, I will arrange the below chapters in a manner that will most effectively introduce the general reader to Tolkien and his works. After surveying Tolkien's biography, noting the people and events in his life that helped form him into the creator of Middle-earth, I will devote most of the book to retelling and analyzing the stories that make up *The Silmarillion, The Hobbit,* and *The Lord of the Rings.*

Though I will often borrow stray insights from the multi-volume history of Middle-earth edited by Christopher Tolkien, I will only single out those that come from Part One of *The Book of Lost Tales* and his stand alone volume, *Unfinished Tales.* In the remaining chapters, I will provide different perspectives on the legendarium by considering Tolkien's academic essays, shorter fiction, and letters.

Because there are many Tolkien fans who know *The Lord of the Rings*[2] well but have found it difficult to break in to *The Silmarillion,* I will devote much of my attention to the latter book, laying a firm foundation, as Tolkien would have wished, for the War of the Ring that ended the Third Age. I urge anyone who has not read *The Lord of the Rings* to

at least watch the Peter Jackson film trilogy before reading this book. Those with a basic working knowledge of *The Lord of the Rings* will get far more out of my chapters on *The Silmarillion* and will then be ready to go deeper with the chapters that follow.

I could write more, but I can already hear the Road beckoning to me, and I must follow it, if I can. I invite you to join me for the journey.

---

2 Throughout this book, I will italicize *The Lord of the Rings.* Although, as the collective name of a trilogy of books (*The Fellowship of the Ring, The Two Towers, The Return of the King*), it is generally written in plain text (as is The Chronicles of Narnia), Tolkien conceived of and wrote *The Lord of the Rings* as a single novel divided into six books. The only reason it was published as a trilogy is that paper in post-WWII Britain was too expensive to allow for a one-thousand-page fantasy novel to make back its printing cost.

ONE

Biography

THOUGH DESTINED TO BE one of England's best and most beloved writers, John Ronald Reuel Tolkien was not born in England, or anywhere else in the British Isles. Rather, he was born to English parents in Bloemfontein, South Africa, on January 3, 1892—not too far, latitudinally speaking, from New Zealand, where his epic fantasy would be realized on film over a century later! His brother Hilary was born two years later in 1894.

Tolkien, who would one day create two of the most fearsome spiders in literature—Ungoliant in *The Silmarillion* and Shelob in *The Lord of the Rings*—almost died from the deadly sting of a tarantula when he was still a baby. He was saved by a heroic nanny who sucked out the poison in time, but one can only wonder if a deeply-buried, subconscious fear of spiders did not find its way into the dark imagination of Shelob's creator.

When he was three years old, Tolkien, who was not thriving in the South African heat, moved with his mother (Mabel) and brother to England. It was hoped that his father would eventually join them, but he died in 1896 and was buried in Bloemfontein, leaving Tolkien, like so many of his future heroes, an orphaned stranger in a strange land.

But there *was* consolation. Rather than live in the city of Birmingham, Mabel, with financial help from her sister May and her husband, was able to settle with her boys outside the city in the rural countryside of Sarehole. It is no exaggeration to say that, for the young Tolkien, Sarehole *was* the Shire, an as-yet unspoiled patch of jolly old England that even boasted a working mill. Throughout the hard years that would follow, his memories of Sarehole would be to him like a memory of Eden.

Starting at an early age, Tolkien was troubled by a recurring dream of the great wave that destroyed Atlantis, a dream that he gave to the character with whom he most identified: Faramir. Though Tolkien hated it when readers made allegorical links between his fantasy novels and the "real" world, the Shire was as strongly based on Sarehole as the rise and fall of Númenor was based on the rise and fall of Atlantis. Indeed, Tolkien wrote that he was only able to exorcize the dream by incorporating it into his legendarium.

In 1900, when Tolkien was eight, his mother and Aunt May made a momentous decision that would change the course of his life. The two women decided together to enter the Catholic Church. Though May's husband forced his wife to return to the Church of England, he could not convince Mabel to do the same. When she remained firm in her new-found faith, he cut her off financially and the rest of her family shunned her.

Without her brother-in-law's support, Mabel was forced to leave Sarehole and move to the suburbs of Birmingham with her boys. Tolkien hated the move and would pine for his lost English idyll with an elegiac sense of nostalgia that pervades all of his work. He, along with his brother, would follow their mother across the Tiber to Rome, and Tolkien would remain a committed Catholic for the rest of his life. In fact, he would come to regard his mother as a long-suffering martyr for their shared faith.

That sense of his mother's martyrdom was sealed in his heart forever when, in 1904, Mabel died of diabetes, a fate that she would likely have avoided had she had the support of her family. Afraid that her family would force her boys to return to the Church of England as they had forced May, Mabel arranged for Tolkien and Hilary to be placed under the guardianship of Father Francis Morgan, a priest who promised Mabel he would raise the boys and see they got a good education, especially the scholarly Tolkien.

Even before his mother's death, Tolkien had demonstrated a facility for languages. As was expected of good schoolboys in those days, he excelled in Latin and Greek and learned French as well; however, his true love was for the Germanic-Scandinavian family of languages: Welsh, Norse, Finnish, Goth, the

Old English (AKA Anglo-Saxon) of *Beowulf,* and the Middle English of Chaucer and *Sir Gawain and the Green Knight.*

Tolkien was no fan of the Norman Invasion of 1066 (the Battle of Hastings) and felt that the imposition of French culture on the older Anglo-Saxon culture had robbed England of her true soul. Unlike Wales, Scotland, Ireland, France, and Germany, England lacked a native mythology: a gap Tolkien determined to fill with his tales of Middle-earth.

From Tolkien's point of view, the legends of King Arthur had been too corrupted by French influence, and Shakespeare's two fairy plays (*A Midsummer Night's Dream* and *The Tempest*) were silly and frivolous. Tolkien even held a ridiculous grudge against Shakespeare for not having the trees of Birnam Wood actually come to Dunsinane in *Macbeth*: this gap Tolkien would also fill by having the Ents march on Isengard!

Although many readers think that Tolkien fashioned the stories of Middle-earth and then fleshed out the stories by inventing languages for his Elves and Dwarves, Hobbits and Men, the truth is exactly the opposite. Tolkien *began* with the languages, carefully working out their grammars and their phonetics and crafting for each a consistent linguistic family tree of place names, personal names, and objects. Only once he had the geographical and dynastic names worked out did he spin tales to give those names a local habitation in which to dwell. The languages were uniquely his, but he did pattern the high Elvish Quenya on Finnish and the common Elvish Sindarin on Welsh.

In addition to learning and inventing languages, there was nothing Tolkien liked more than starting clubs where he could enjoy good male friendships, vigorous conversation, and warm pipes and beer. The most enduring of those clubs earned the rather lengthy name of the Tea Club Barrovian Society, or T.C.B.S. for short. Though members came and went, the group soon formed

itself around an inseparable inner circle they called the Immortal Four: Tolkien, Christopher Wiseman, Robert Gilson, and G. B. Smith.

Far more than a group of friends meeting for drinks, the T.C.B.S. felt themselves called to restore beauty, goodness, and truth to a cynical, decadent age. Though they were by no means puritanical, they longed to see moral reform in England. They believed strongly in duty and patriotism but were not big defenders of the British Empire. Their love, like the Hobbits' love for the Shire, was a local and tangible love for home and land and family.

Such were the male friends of the man who would one day structure an epic fantasy around a fellowship of nine male friends. Still, fate had in store for Tolkien a remarkable woman who would exert a profound influence on his life and work. Her name was Edith Bratt, and she was, like Tolkien, an orphan. They met in a boardinghouse in 1908, when Tolkien was sixteen and Edith was nineteen.

Tolkien quickly fell in love with Edith and began to date her. When Father Francis found out, he was not pleased: partly because she was Protestant, but just as much because he feared she would distract Tolkien from his studies and prevent him from achieving the academic scores he needed to win a scholarship from Oxford. To give Father Francis his due, the first time Tolkien took his exams, he did not get a high enough score—likely because he was spending so much time with Edith.

Francis, who was still Tolkien's legal guardian, forced his young ward to break up with her. Tolkien, not one to be dissuaded, saw her several more times in secret. Alas, the clandestine lovers were caught two more times, and, in the end, Francis made Tolkien promise him that he would not speak or write to Edith until he reached the legal age of twenty-one. Tolkien's

love for Edith was strong, but he also had a strong sense of respect and duty for the man who was both his mother's appointed guardian and a Catholic priest. In the end, he reluctantly agreed to Francis's terms.

But the story does not end there! The moment his twenty-first birthday arrived, Tolkien made an intense search for the girl whom he had not communicated with for three years. As soon as he located her address, he went to her and proposed. In the interim, Edith had gotten engaged, but when Tolkien proposed, she broke the engagement, converted to Catholicism, and married her first love. They went on to raise three sons (John, who became a priest, Michael, and Christopher) and one daughter (Priscilla) and remained faithfully married until Edith's death in 1971.

Tolkien's troubled love affair with Edith found its way into the very heart of his legendarium, inspiring the tragic love story of Beren the Man and Lúthien the Elf, a match that Lúthien's strong-willed father tries to destroy before eventually giving in. To make the tale even more personal, Tolkien has Beren fall in love with Lúthien in the same way that he fell in love with Edith—when they saw their future beloved singing and dancing in a meadow under a tree.

I will tell the story of Beren and Lúthien in chapter three. For now, let it suffice to note that after Edith died, Tolkien crafted the headstone that still stands over their graves. On it are engraved three things: their names, their dates, and the names Beren and Lúthien.

Before he married Edith in 1916, Tolkien attended and graduated (in 1915) from Exeter College, Oxford, where he focused on pre-Chaucer language and literature. His marriage was followed shortly after by his deployment to France, where he fought in, and survived, the bloody Battle of the Somme. The horrors he saw in WWI, especially the rotting corpses in the bleak and desolate hell hole of no man's land, would stay with him forever and influence his descriptions of the Dead Marshes and the starved and wasted land of Mordor.

Two good things, however, came out of the war. First, one of Tolkien's duties was to break in new warhorses, a job that increased his love for those majestic animals. His work with horses likely inspired him in his creation of the Rohirrim, the horse-riding Men of Rohan. Tolkien clearly modeled the Rohirrim on the Anglo-Saxon warriors of *Beowulf,* who sing in the same alliterative verse in which *Beowulf* was composed and who feast together in a great mead-hall. But then he factored in one significant addition. Whereas the warriors who appear in *Beowulf* do not fight on horseback, the Rohirrim do!

Second, Tolkien found that he preferred the company of the humbler private soldiers to that of his fellow officers. Many of those private soldiers also served as batmen, servants who saw to the daily, domestic needs of the officers. Tolkien would base the character of Sam Gamgee, Frodo's loyal and resourceful gardener, on the batmen that he came to know, love, and respect during his years in the trenches.

Tolkien would likely have died in France had he not contracted trench fever from the lice that infested the constantly muddy barracks. Neither Gilson nor Smith proved so lucky; both died on the battlefields of what Europeans still refer to as the Great War. Wiseman survived, but the noble T.C.B.S. was gone. Though Tolkien named his son Christopher after Wiseman, the two remaining members of the Immortal Four slowly drifted apart.

In his biography, *Tolkien*, Humphrey Carpenter titles chapter eight, the chapter that recounts the death of Smith and Gilson, "The breaking of the fellowship." He closes the chapter by quoting a letter that Gilson sent to Tolkien a few days before he was killed at the Battle of the Somme. It contains this charge to the future author of *The Lord of the Rings*:

"My chief consolation is that if I am scuppered tonight . . . there will still be left a member of the great T.C.B.S. to voice what I dreamed and what we all agreed upon. For the death of one of its members cannot, I am determined, dissolve the T.C.B.S. Death can make us loathsome and helpless as individuals, but it cannot put an end to the immortal four! . . . May God bless you my dear John Ronald and may you say things I have tried to say long after I am not there to say them if such be my lot."

Tolkien would live up to Smith's challenge. As he was moved from one hospital to the next—for each time he was ordered to return to the front, his trench fever broke out again—he set himself to writing down many of the stories that would eventually be collected and published posthumously by his son Christopher as *The Silmarillion*.

For most Englishmen, WWI finished off the whole notion of epic or heroic literature and caused the genre of fantasy to be relegated to the nursery. There were some writers, like George Orwell, Kurt Vonnegut, and William Golding, who, in the 1940s and 50s, wrote in the mode of fantasy, but their works were deeply ironic and ultimately anti-heroic. Tolkien, without falling into the other extreme of escapist fiction, pressed on in the spirit of the T.C.B.S. to fashion a new epic that was elegiac but hopeful, filled with the grim realities of war and loss but illuminated by courage, faith, and camaraderie.

While Tolkien went on to live the petite bourgeois life of a Hobbit, traveling little and maintaining his simple taste in food and clothing, he chose to send his heroes on adventures that took them far from home and tested their moral fiber. Though he at one time possessed a car, he eventually got rid of it and never drove again! To his children he proved a loving and involved father. He even wrote them an increasingly complex and multi-layered series of letters from the North Pole, whimsical and wildly imaginative letters that would be published posthumously as *Letters from Father Christmas*.

After WWI, Tolkien's reputation as a gifted student of language was already so strong that he was selected to work on the Oxford English Dictionary (OED); he was assigned words beginning with "W." In 1920, he was appointed Reader in English Language at Leeds

University, and, two years later, got to work alongside the great E. V. Gordon on the translation of and notes for *Sir Gawain and the Green Knight*. Later, he would work on two other poems in the same dialect of Middle English: *Pearl* and *Sir Orfeo*.

In 1925, Tolkien's hard work and deep insight into language—it was said of him that he had gotten *inside* language—bore full fruit when he was elected Professor of Anglo-Saxon at Oxford. Were a thirty-three-year-old professor to be awarded a professorship today it would be quite a feat; back in the 1920s, it was almost unheard of! Better yet, in 1945, he earned even greater prestige by being elected the Merton Professor of English Language and Literature at Oxford.

Though many today imagine that Tolkien was a linguist, he was, in fact, a philologist. The distinction is a vital one. Whereas the former approach language from the point of view of an evolutionary scientist, the latter approach it from that of a humanistic lover of literature. For Tolkien, words are not arbitrary scratches or sounds; neither are they signifiers trapped in a self-referential and finally self-consuming linguistic system. To the contrary, they are concrete, meaningful, and alive. They point to real goodness, truth, and beauty, even as they incarnate the culture and myths and dreams of a people.

It was this love of language and its story-telling, truth-conveying power that led Tolkien to deliver, in 1936, a famous, paradigm-shifting lecture: "*Beowulf*: The Monsters and the Critics." At the time, most scholars treated *Beowulf* as a linguistic and historical artifact. Tolkien forced them to consider it as a poem, as a work of art, genius, and inspiration. Indeed, he argued that the art is so good, most who read it cannot help but interpret it as a historical work—leading them, ironically, to treat it as an artifact instead of a work of art!

It took some courage for Tolkien to deliver his lecture, but by then he had gained the support of a fellow Oxford don who, in his own way, took the place of the T.C.B.S. His name was C. S. Lewis, and the two men met in 1926, drawn together by their mutual love of all things Norse and their shared desire to see Oxford maintain a proper

balance between the study of literature and the study of ancient (dead) languages.

By then, Tolkien, with his inveterate skill for starting groups, had established a special club known as the Coalbiters. The purpose of the club was to read out loud the Icelandic sagas in their original languages; in fact, the name of the group was a reference to the Vikings who sat so close to the fire as they shared their heroic tales that they seemed to be biting the coals. Lewis quickly joined the group and stayed with it until it folded—due to the fact that they had worked their way through all of the sagas!

When the two men met, Lewis was an atheist, who, though he loved the literature of the Middle Ages, had rejected its Christian beliefs. Were it not for the influence of Tolkien, Lewis might never have embraced the faith that led him to write some of the most enduring works of Christian apologetics (*The Problem of Pain, Miracles, Mere*

Christianity, The Screwtape Letters, The Great Divorce), science-fiction (The Space Trilogy), and fantasy (*Till We Have Faces* and the beloved Chronicles of Narnia).

Though other events and people helped lead Lewis to a belief in God, it was Tolkien who played the central role in nudging him from theism to Christianity. The love for myth that Lewis shared with Tolkien had convinced him that Jesus was merely the Hebrew version of an age-old myth in which a demigod came to earth, died, and returned to the heavens in sympathy with the seasonal cycle of life, death, and rebirth.

One night in 1931, while the two men, together with their mutual friend Hugo Dyson, walked along a tree-lined path on the grounds of Magdalen College, Oxford, Tolkien challenged Lewis to re-examine his belief that Christ was *only* a myth. What if, Tolkien suggested, the reason that Jesus sounded like a myth was because he was the myth that came true? It was this suggestion, that Jesus Christ was the true myth, that the grand story that seems to have been inscribed in the DNA of all the ancient nations had actually happened once in real time and space, that threw open the closed doors of Lewis's heart.

Many years later, Lewis wrote an essay on what Tolkien had taught him that he titled "Myth Became Fact." As for Tolkien, when, in 1939, he delivered a lecture titled "On Fairy-stories," he ended it by presenting the gospel message as the grand story, or metanarrative, that lies behind all the best fairy tales. Since the more private Tolkien was more reticent than Lewis about mentioning his faith directly in his work, his comments tend to surprise readers, especially if they are not aware of the depth and strength of Tolkien's Catholicism. That the comments appear at all bears testimony to how important the concept of Christianity as a true myth was to the Catholic creator of Middle-earth.

Though Tolkien was disappointed that Lewis chose to remain in the Anglican Church of his upbringing rather than convert to

Catholicism, the two shared a deep commitment to Christianity and attracted to themselves a coterie of other scholarly and/or creative Christian men: among them, Owen Barfield, Hugo Dyson, Nevill Coghill, Lewis's brother Warren, and, later, Charles Williams and Tolkien's son Christopher.

Beginning in 1933, this happy band met together weekly in a local pub called The Eagle and Child (or Bird and Baby or B&B) to share their mutual passions and to read out loud whatever new essay or book they had been writing. To facilitate the serious reading and critiquing of each other's work, they also met once a week in Lewis's rooms in Magdalen. They called themselves the Inklings, not only because they spilled a lot of ink, but because they all, in their own way, were haunted by intimations of greater goodness, truth, and beauty. Many a fan of Lewis and Tolkien has wished he could have been a fly on the wall to witness one of their meetings!

Lord Cecil · Hugo Dyson · CS Lewis · Charles Williams

THE INKLINGS (some of them)

Unlike Lewis, who published book after book on a variety of different topics, Tolkien was at once a procrastinator and a perfectionist who found it hard to finish projects that he had begun. This was as true for his scholarly work as it was for the many fantasy stories that he would start and then abandon. But there was one children's story that he *did* finish, a work that would have a lasting impact, not only on Tolkien, but on the future history of children's literature and fantasy.

The name of that work is *The Hobbit*, and Tolkien would publish it to popular and critical acclaim in 1937. *The Hobbit* takes place in the Third Age of the imaginative world that Tolkien had conceived in his teens but began writing in earnest during his period of WWI convalescence. But with one major addition. The stories that would later be published as *The Silmarillion* contained Valar, Maiar, Elves, Men, and Dwarves, but no Hobbits.

Those small, furry-footed, food-loving farmers would spring into existence in Tolkien's mind while he was grading a stack of exam papers. For some reason that must remain a part of that great mystery we call inspiration, Tolkien wrote a sentence in a blank page of one of the exams: "In a hole in the ground there lived a hobbit." That sentence, which would become the famous opening line of *The Hobbit*, would send Tolkien on his own literary journey to discover what Hobbits are and what they do.

About the same time, Lewis and Tolkien had been taking one of their regular walks and discussing a topic that was dear to both of their hearts: why was it that no one was writing good fantasy literature for adults? This time, however, their conversation, rather than ending with a passive shrug of the shoulders, ended with the decision that they would have to write the kinds of books they wanted to read.

Lewis agreed to take up space travel and followed through by writing *Out of the Silent Planet* (1938), the first installment in his Space Trilogy. Tolkien agreed to take up time travel and started a work called *The Lost Road* that would allow him to incorporate the tales he had already written during WWI of the First Age of Middle-earth. Alas, as was so often the case with Tolkien, he never finished it. Still, it is likely that the challenge played some role in his writing of *The Hobbit*.

Indeed, speaking more generally, there would have been no *Hobbit* or *Lord of the Rings* were in not for the friendship of Lewis and the support of the Inklings. Although all of the Inklings were Christian, and though Christianity frequently came up as a topic, their meetings were neither Bible studies nor forums for discussions of faith. They met to encourage and critique each other's work, and, since many of them were writing in genres (fantasy, science-fiction, children's literature) that were no longer taken seriously by academics and critics, that encouragement and critique was essential to their morale.

Lewis and Tolkien had grown up in the Golden Age of imaginative fiction meant for the delight of children and adults alike: *The Jungle Book*, *The Wind in the Willows*, *Alice in Wonderland*, and the writings of Beatrix Potter, Edith Nesbit, and George MacDonald. After WWI, however, a cynical and embittered Europe turned away from literature they now saw as unrealistic, sentimental, and escapist. The support and constructive criticism provided by the Inklings helped writers like Tolkien and Lewis to persevere in writing the kinds of books that they—but seemingly nobody else—wanted to read.

Thankfully, the success of *The Hobbit* proved that the English reading public *was* ready to embrace again fantasy literature with the power to provoke wonder, awe, and joy in child and adult readers. In fact, so successful was the book that the publishers began to push Tolkien for a sequel. The time had come, Tolkien thought to himself, to publish the heroic but tragic tales he had already written about the First Age of Middle-earth.

But that was not to be! *The Silmarillion* would have to await publication until after the death of its author for one simple reason—it had no Hobbits in it. And what the publisher, and the reading public, wanted was more Hobbits like the loveable Bilbo Baggins. That meant great frustration for Tolkien but great luck for the rest of the world. For what makes *The Lord of the Rings* so unique is that it fuses perfectly the heavy, epic, elegiac mood of *The Silmarillion* with the light, whimsical, hopeful mood of *The Hobbit*.

It is precisely that balance of high and low, darkness and light, of the tragic and the comic, the somber and the merry, the world-weary and the innocent that makes *The Lord of the Rings* so unique in its tone and ethos. And it is the Hobbits who hold it all together, for they are willing to face every manner of danger, deprivation, and despair to preserve the simple life of the Shire and its jolly and industrious, if somewhat self-satisfied and over-fed, inhabitants.

But the creation of *The Lord of the Rings* was no easy matter. It took Tolkien a full twelve years (1937-1949) to write his epic. For much of that time, it was only Lewis and his son Christopher who gave Tolkien the motivation he needed to keep calm and carry on. We are lucky to possess some first-hand accounts of Tolkien's epic labors in the letters he wrote to Christopher during his son's military service in WWII, letters in which he frequently fills his son in on how composition on *The Lord of the Rings* is going.

One of the most exciting bits about these on-the-ground, hot-off-the-presses reports of Tolkien's literary progress is that they occasionally include a paragraph in which Tolkien writes that a character has just arrived on the scene, and he is not sure what to do with him. Tolkien often claimed that he was more an editor than an inventor of the tales of Middle-earth; these letters bear witness that Tolkien's claim was a sincere one.

Here, for example, is a passage from his May 4, 1944, letter to his son: "A new character has come on the scene (I am sure I did not invent him, I did not even want him though I like him, but there he came walking into the woods of Ithilien): Faramir, the brother of Boromir." When Tolkien wrote this, he had no idea *The Lord of the Rings* would be a sensation or that his letters would be published. That is to say, there is no reason to doubt he was telling the truth when he described Faramir as pushing his way into the story.

One of the reasons that readers take *The Lord of the Rings* so seriously, with so many of them judging it the best book of the twentieth century, is that it seems to have a reality apart from its author. The engaged reader cannot help but feel that Tolkien is less a fantasy author than a scribe or chronicler of a history he has been allowed to glimpse, a feeling that grows stronger when one reads the various fragments of the legendarium that Christopher devoted over forty years of his life to uncovering, editing, and publishing.

I said a moment ago that Tolkien completed *The Lord of the Rings* in 1949, but it would take another five years to find its way into print. Much of that delay was due to Tolkien being something of a curmudgeon. He fought with his publisher and editors over the look and length of the novel and its inclusion of maps and illustrations, at least one of which he wanted in color. And he kept trying to sneak in the Hobbit-less *Silmarillion*.

To make matters worse, the publisher, due to the high cost of post-WWII paper, insisted, much to Tolkien's dismay, that his single, six-book epic be broken into three shorter novels. In the end, he grudgingly agreed, and *The Fellowship of the Ring* and *The Two Towers* were published in 1954, followed by *The Return of the King* in 1955.

Most academics and literary critics refused, and continued to refuse for many decades, to take Tolkien's epic fantasy seriously, but support did come in from such writers as W. H. Auden, Iris Murdoch, Naomi Mitchison, and, of course, C. S. Lewis. Lewis even put his academic reputation on the line by writing a celebratory review of *The Lord of the Rings* that hailed it as a supreme work of mythmaking redolent with history and a deep knowledge of human nature in its joy and its anguish, its hope and its despair.

Sadly, though Lewis never wavered in his support for *The Lord of the Rings*, Tolkien never warmed up to Lewis's Chronicles of Narnia, considering them too allegorical, too inconsistent, and too hastily written. To be fair to Lewis's fantasy series, it must be admitted that Creation, when compared to Tolkien's legendarium, was a decidedly slap-dash affair. God, after all, only had a week to work with!

Tolkien would have to deal with pirated American editions of his epic, and he never really knew what to make of the cultic fans on both sides of the Atlantic who obsessed over his work. Still, he patiently answered letters from fans and even took time to write a very long letter, filled with sensible advice, to an American company that wanted to adapt *The Lord of the Rings* into an animated film. Though he never did find a publisher for *The Silmarillion*, he was able, before his death in 1973, to publish three fantasy stories and a delightful collection of poems that featured his quirkiest creation, Tom Bombadil.

Tolkien retired in 1959 and lived out a long, peaceful, Hobbit-like retirement that would have pleased the most bourgeois of adventurers, Bilbo Baggins.

Works by Tolkien published during his lifetime:

1936	*"Beowulf: The Monsters and the Critics"*
1937	*The Hobbit*
1949	*Farmer Giles of Ham*
1954	*The Fellowship of the Ring* and *The Two Towers*
1955	*The Return of the King*
1962	*The Adventures of Tom Bombadil*
1964	*Tree and Leaf* ("On Fairy-stories" + "Leaf by Niggle")
1967	*Smith of Wootton Major*

Books by Tolkien edited and published posthumously by Christopher Tolkien (*Letters from Father Christmas* was edited by his second wife, Baillie Tolkien):

1975	*Translations of Sir Gawain, Pearl, and Sir Orfeo*
1976	*Letters from Father Christmas*
1977	*The Silmarillion*
1980	*Unfinished Tales of Númenor and Middle-earth*
1981	*Letters of J. R. R. Tolkien*
1983	*The Monsters and the Critics, and Other Essays*
1983	*Book of Lost Tales I (The History of Middle-earth 1)*
1984	*Book of Lost Tales II (The History of Middle-earth 2)*
1985	*Lays of Beleriand (The History of Middle-earth 3)*
1986–96	*Volumes 4–12 of The History of Middle-earth*
2007	*The Children of Húrin*
2009	*The Legend of Sigurd and Gudrún*
2013	*The Fall of Arthur*
2014	*Beowulf: A Translation and Commentary*
2017	*Beren and Lúthien*
2018	*The Fall of Gondolin*

TWO

The Silmarillion I: In the Beginning

The eternal, omnipotent, omniscient God is known as **Eru** (the One) or **Ilúvatar** (Father of All).

He creates a race of angelic beings known as the **Ainur**.
Those who choose to live on Arda are called **Valar**, the Powers of the World.
The four chief Valar can be linked to the four elements:
Air: **Manwë**, whose consort is **Varda** (**Elbereth** to the Elves);
Earth: **Aulë**, whose consort is **Yavanna**;
Water: **Ulmo**, who has no consort;
Fire: **Melkor** (**Morgoth** to the Elves), who has no consort.
Mandos fulfils the role of Hades, guardian of the dead.

They are served by a race of lesser angels known as the **Maiar:**
Sauron is a Maia of Aulë who is corrupted by Melkor;
The **Balrogs** are corrupted Maiar in the form of fire demons;
Dragons are corrupted Maiar as is the spider **Ungoliant**.
Wizards (or **Istari**) like **Gandalf** and **Saruman** are also Maiar.

Arda is home to a number of rational creatures:
Elves are the firstborn: beautiful, immortal, and sad;
Men are given the gift of mortality, which makes them restless;
Dwarves are fashioned by Aulë but given life by Ilúvatar;
Yavanna makes talking **Eagles** and trees (**Ents**) to protect nature.

THE TALE

In the beginning, Eru (the One), who has always been and who is known as Ilúvatar (the Father of All), created space, time, and matter out of his eternal thoughts. He then set his mind to the making of spiritual beings whom he called the Ainur and on whom he bestowed a great gift. As Ilúvatar set out to sing into being Arda (our earth), he granted to the Ainur the great privilege of joining him in his song.

But Melkor, the greatest and most beautiful of the Ainur, grew proud in his heart and desired to sing a song of his own that did not come from the mind of Ilúvatar. And so he exerted all his power and skill to dominate and shape the song to his own perverse design. Great evil would come of his pride, but he could not defeat the song of Ilúvatar. Each time he injected his twisted and ugly strains into the song, Ilúvatar wove them back into his own song, thus increasing its complexity and beauty.

Besides, Melkor did not understand that he and his fellow Ainur knew only a part of the song of creation, and, of that, only the geography and the plant and animal life of Arda. Ilúvatar alone knew the full song and its proper ending, and Ilúvatar alone fashioned the Elves and the Men who would rule over the land and creatures. And none but Ilúvatar knew the Secret Fire by which he created, though Melkor burned to know and possess it.

Slowly, strain by strain, the song was composed, assembled, and orchestrated. Only once it reached perfection as a song did Ilúvatar say, "Ea" ("let it be"), and Arda, in all its beauty, rose out of the primal chaos of the

34

void to inhabit space and time. All the Ainur rejoiced, but there were some that so loved Arda that they chose to descend and so be bound to the life and fate of Arda. Those who chose were henceforth called the Valar.

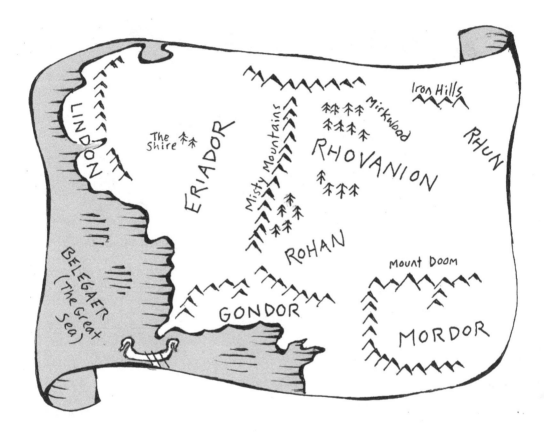

Ilúvatar chose Manwë, Lord of the Air, to rule over Arda with his queen, Varda, the Lady of Stars and Light, whom the Elves named Elbereth. He was assisted by Aulë, Lord of the Earth, whose consort Yavanna was queen of all the things that grow. Ulmo, who lived alone, was Lord of the Sea, the part of Arda in which the song of creation lived on in its original purity. Alas, Melkor, too, the rebellious Lord of Fire, chose to be a Valar.

To serve the Valar, Ilúvatar appointed the Maiar, angelic beings who were of the same kind as the Valar but lesser in degree. Like the Valar, they were given free will, most of whom used it for good, but some of whom used it for evil. Sauron, a Maia of Aulë, was seduced by Melkor and joined him in his anger, envy, and destructive greed for power.

Above all things, Melkor hated the water and the light. He fought their healing power by corrupting other Maiar who took on the forms of Dragons, fire demons (the Balrogs), and spiders (Ungoliant). In later years, he perverted Elves into Orcs and Ents into Trolls.

36

The Istari (or Wizards) were Maiar who took on the form of old, bearded Men. Two of them, Gandalf and Radagast, would help Middle-earth in her time of greatest need, but Saruman would be corrupted by Sauron and by his own lust to dominate and control.

Before the sun and moon were created, during the innocent spring of Arda, the Valar lived in Middle-earth, the inhabited realms of Arda that would later house Elves and Dwarves, Hobbits and Men. In answer to a prayer of Yavanna, Aulë created two lamps to warm and illumine Middle-earth, but Melkor, in his evil, destroyed the lamps.

As a result, the Valar left Middle-earth and dwelt far to the west in the misty, undying lands of Valinor. There, Yavanna sang a song of exquisite beauty that caused Two Trees of silver (Telperion) and gold

(Laurelin) to grow out of the earth. The Trees gave both light and life to Valinor and began the count of time.

It was at this time that the firstborn children of Ilúvatar, the Elves, came to life in the empty lands of Middle-earth.

They were known as well as the Eldar, the People of the Stars, and they were immortal beings who did not wax old or grow sick and die. They could be killed by violence, but if they were, they would sink down to the Halls of Mandos, where they would be reborn and return to Middle-earth.

Though immortal, the lives of the Eldar were bound inextricably to the life of Arda. Men, in contrast, who would not be born until the creation of the sun and the moon, were given by Ilúvatar the gift of mortality. This gift was a pledge that their final destiny lay beyond the confines of the world, but it was a gift that made them restless and filled them with a desire to perform deeds of note that would be remembered.

As for the Dwarves, their birth was not a part of the original song of Ilúvatar. Aulë, impatient to meet the Elves and wanting to have creatures of his own to care for, fashioned the Dwarves out of the earth, making them less beautiful than Elves but stronger and more hearty. When Ilúvatar discovered what Aulë had done, he was filled with wrath and rebuked the impatient Valar.

In response, Aulë lifted his hammer to smash the creatures he had made, who as yet lacked life and consciousness. But Ilúvatar pitied the Dwarves and granted them the life that Aulë could not give them, though he put them temporarily under the earth so they would not come to life before the Elves, whom he had decreed would be the firstborn.

My beard is beautiful

39

When Yavanna learned of the Dwarves, she feared that they would lay waste to the nature she so loved. To protect nature, she fashioned the Ents, herders of the Trees who can move through the earth and speak, and Eagles, magnificent birds who possess, as well, the power of rational thought and of speech.

DIGGING DEEPER

Genesis alone of ancient books says that a single God created the world out of nothing (*ex nihilo* in Latin). In the myths of the Greeks, Romans, Egyptians, Babylonians, Scandinavians, Chinese, Indians, Native Americans, and so forth, matter comes first, and the gods evolve *out of it*. During the early centuries of Christianity, many Gnostic sects sprang up that accepted that spirit came before matter but that treated the creation of the earth (and the physical body) as a mistake, the aborted experiment of a lesser deity.

Tolkien follows Genesis in positing an eternal God who creates *ex nihilo* and calls his creation good. Tolkien, however, has God sing (rather than speak) creation into being, and he has God allow the angelic beings he created to participate in the song. (Influenced by Tolkien, C. S. Lewis has his Christ-figure, the Lion Aslan, sing Narnia into being in *The Magician's Nephew!*) But the Ilúvatar of *The Silmarillion* and *The Lord of the Rings* does not reveal himself directly to Elves or Men as he does in the Bible. That is because Tolkien's tales take place in pre-historical time, before God revealed himself to Abraham.

In one of his letters, Tolkien explains that we are living at the end of the Fifth Age. Since Ages tend to be about 3,000 years in length, and since *The Lord of the Rings* takes place at the end of the Third Age, the final defeat of Sauron occurs sometime before 4004 BC, the traditional date for the creation as calculated by Bishop Ussher. That means

Tolkien's tales are not only pre-Christian; they are pre-Jewish as well.

Though Tolkien avoids one-to-one correspondences between our world and his invented, pre-historical world, Melkor is clearly a satanic figure. Like the Lucifer of the Bible (and *Paradise Lost!*), he was once an Angel of Light who gave way to pride and refused to obey his Creator. He will neither serve nor follow in the melodies and harmonies initiated by Ilúvatar. But the connection between Satan and Melkor goes deeper than that.

Just as the wiles of the devil were used by God to bring about a greater good and to shower even more grace upon his creatures, so all the attempts of Melkor to spoil the song of Ilúvatar are used *by* Ilúvatar for greater good and beauty. Thus, the rebellion of Melkor acts as a *felix culpa* (Latin for "happy fault"), an evil out of which good arises. Even so did the horror of the Crucifixion give way to the triumph of the Resurrection.

According to I Peter I, prophets and angels alike searched and yearned for knowledge of God's promised gospel (good news), his gracious plan for saving fallen mankind. In Tolkien's legendarium, neither Elves nor Men nor Valar can conceive of the plans of Ilúvatar that will someday be enacted in the time and space of Arda.

Though Tolkien's vision tends to be more Norse than Greek—Ainur likely comes from Aesir, the Norse gods who dwell at Asgard—his pantheon of Valar cleaves more closely to the gods of Greek mythology, with Manwë, Ulmo, Mandos, and Aulë resembling Zeus, Poseidon, Hades, and Hephaestus. Biblical imagery, however, also plays a part. Manwë is as much like Zeus as he is like the Archangel Michael, who defends Israel and leads the armies of God against Satan. Elbereth, meanwhile, is the Virgin Mary-like Queen of Heaven, though Galadriel also embodies Mary, but in a more earthly way.

Like the angels of the Bible, the Valar are spirit beings who take on physical form to appear on the earth—not, to be sure, like the fully incarnate Christ, but like a man who puts on a suit of clothes that reveals his personality. In the First Age, they walked often in Middle-earth, but after that they withdrew to Valinor in the West and were seen no more.

Free will plays a vital role in Tolkien's legendarium. For Tolkien, nothing is evil in the beginning, not even Melkor, but it can choose to turn from the good and become perverse. Ossë, a Maia of Ulmo, was, like Sauron, corrupted by Melkor, but, in the end, he repented and was restored to fellowship. Like Lewis, Tolkien agreed with St. Augustine that evil is not a positive thing but a negation (or privation) of the good.

It is important to understand that Elves are immortal but not eternal. They are created beings and do not exist outside of time and space as does Ilúvatar. It is equally important to understand that physical death in Tolkien is not, like spiritual death, a result of the Fall but a gift of God to Men. We are not destined, like the Elves, to be confined forever to the cycles of Arda but are meant to escape to a higher kind of life—though what that higher life is to be is not revealed in the legendarium.

Finally, in an overt biblical connection, Tolkien links the Secret Fire, which Melkor can neither possess nor understand, to the Holy Spirit that hovered over the waters of creation (Genesis 1:2). It is that Fire that Gandalf will call upon to defeat the Balrog in Moria.

"But now Ilúvatar sat and hearkened, and for a great while it seemed good to him, for in the music there were no flaws. But as the theme progressed, it came into the heart of Melkor to interweave matters of his own imagining that were not in accord with the theme of Ilúvatar, for he sought therein to increase the power and glory of the part assigned to himself" (*The Silmarillion, Ainulindalë*).

"Thus it came to pass that of the Ainur some abode still with Ilúvatar beyond the confines of the World; but others, and among them many of the greatest and most fair, took the leave of Ilúvatar and descended into it. But this condition Ilúvatar made, or it is the necessity of their love, that their power should thenceforward be contained and bounded in the World, to be within it for ever, until it is complete, so that they are its life and it is theirs. And therefore they are named the Valar, the Powers of the World" (*The Silmarillion, Ainulindalë*).

THREE

The Silmarillion II: The Coming of the Noldor

The fiery **Fëanor**, son of **Finwe**, is the greatest of the **Noldor**
Elves;
His seven sons include **Maedhros**, **Celegorm**, and **Curufin**.

To his half-brother **Fingolfin** is born three children:
Sons **Fingon** and **Turgon** and daughter **Aredhel**.
Fingon is father of **Gil-Galad** and Turgon of **Idril**;
Aredhel foolishly weds the Dark Elf **Eöl** and bears **Maeglin**.

Fingolfin's brother **Finarfin** fathers five children:
Among them sons **Finrod** and **Orodreth** and daughter
Galadriel.

THE TALE

Now the Elves were born under the stars in the fields of Middle-earth
after the Valar had abandoned them for Valinor in the west. The place
of their birth was not pristine, as it had been during the spring of Arda,
but was marred by the treachery and malice of Melkor who hated life
and beauty and sought ever to corrupt and undo what Ilúvatar or the
Valar had built. He warred too with the Elves, hating them, as he
would later hate Men, for they were the Children of Ilúvatar, creations
of his personal song.

Tired of their long struggles with Melkor, many of the Elves, most notably the Noldor and the Teleri, chose to leave Middle-earth and seek out the peace and protection of Valinor. Of all the Valar, Ulmo most loved the Elves, so much so that he fashioned for them an island-boat to ferry them across the sea to Valinor. Once there, the island put down roots off the coast of Valinor and was known as Tol Eressëa, the Lonely Isle.

For many long years, the Elves and Valar lived together in harmony, and Arda was blessed with a second spring. But it was not to last. The Valar had captured and bound Melkor for his evil deeds, but the wily Lord of Fire had deceived the innocent Valar, convincing them that he had repented of his evil ways. No sooner did he return to Valinor than he began to corrupt the Noldor, promising them forbidden knowledge and breeding in them mistrust and resentment of the Valar.

Now a Noldor Elf named Finwe fathered Fëanor with his first wife and Fingolfin and Finarfin with his second. The eldest of the three was an Elf of great courage and skill, but he was also fiery and possessive and easily moved to wrath. Being, like all the Noldor, a master of gems, he found a way to take the divine light from the Two Trees and incarnate it in three crystal globes that he called the Silmarils.

The Valar applauded Fëanor's skill, but Melkor lusted to possess the Silmarils for himself, even though he hated and was pained by the light that shone within them. Fëanor refused to surrender even one of the three Silmarils, and so Melkor sought help from Ungoliant, a fierce Maia in the form of a giant spider whose hatred of light and life exceeded that of Melkor himself.

One day, as the Valar celebrated a festival, Melkor and Ungoliant made their way in secret to the Two Trees, which the unsuspecting Valar had left unguarded. As Melkor hewed the sacred branches and trunks, Ungoliant sucked the light of the Trees into her ravenous belly. They then rushed to the camp of the Noldor, where they killed Finwe and stole all the gems they found, including the three Silmarils. Ungoliant devoured the gems to feed her endless, unquenchable hunger, but Melkor kept the Silmarils for himself.

The two villains then fled far to the north where a snowy waste-land known as Helcaraxë, the Grinding Ice, united the coast of Valinor with the far west of Middle-earth, lands that now lie under the sea, but were then called Beleriand. In the northernmost reaches of Beleriand, in the region of Angband, Melkor built Thangorodrim, an impregnable fortress honeycombed with pits where he twisted Elves into Orcs and forged weapons of war.

As for Ungoliant, she found a new home in the mountains that lay just south of Angband. There in Ered Gorgoroth, the Mountains of Terror, she spun her webs and gave birth to a brood of evil spiders who troubled the land. Of this brood came Shelob the Great.

Meanwhile, in Valinor, the Valar grieved the loss of the Trees and their divine light that lived now only in the Silmarils. To compensate for the loss of that light, they fashioned the sun and the moon, under whose light Men would, in keeping with Ilúvatar's song, be born. They begged the Noldor to remain in Valinor with them and seek solace together, but Fëanor swore a terrible oath that he would not rest until he had taken back the Silmarils from Melkor. He then forced his seven sons to swear the oath as well.

Ignoring the Valar's warnings, Fëanor and his sons set out north in pursuit of Melkor. With him went Fingolfin and his two sons and daughter, accompanied by the four sons and daughter of Finarfin. On the way, they came to Alqualondë, a coastal settlement of Teleri Elves who had lived on Tol Eressëa and been taught shipbuilding by Ulmo.

Fëanor asked the Teleri to give him ships so that he might sail across the sea to Beleriand, but the Teleri refused to help Elves who had disobeyed the Valar. In a fit of rage, Fëanor attacked the Teleri, shedding the blood of many and stealing their ships. This was the first kin-slaying of the Elves, and it led the Valar to put a deadly curse on Fëanor and his kin.

Rather than repent of his ill deeds, Fëanor, driven by his oath, committed yet another. Since there were not enough Teleri ships to ferry all the Elves across the sea, he sailed with his sons and retainers, promising to send the ships back to ferry the rest. Instead, when he reached Beleriand, he burned the ships to prevent contenders for the Silmarils.

When the families of Fingolfin and Finarfin saw the smoke rising in the east, they knew they had been betrayed. Rather than return to Valinor, however, they made their way on foot through Helcaraxë. It was a bitter journey, and many died along the way. When the Elves were gone, the Valar hid Valinor away and decreed the Noldor could never return. Thus the Doom of the Noldor, known also as the Curse of Mandos, fell upon the Elves.

Once in Middle-earth, the Noldor spread out and set up their camps across Beleriand: all but Fëanor. His oath burned within him, and he led a brave but foolhardy assault on Thangorodrim, during which he was mortally wounded by a Balrog. He knew the power of the Noldor could not defeat Thangorodrim alone; nevertheless, with his last breath, he cursed Morgoth and made his sons swear to avenge him and stay true to their oath. Then, consumed by the inner fury of his fiery heart, his body fell to ash, and he was no more.

It was Fëanor who changed the name of Melkor to Morgoth, the Black Enemy, and it was by that name, and that name alone, that he would forever be known in Middle-earth.

Driven to ruin by their father's oath, the sons of Fëanor attacked

Morgoth, and Maedhros, the eldest son, was captured. In an act of great love and honor, Fingon, eldest son of Fingolfin, put aside the rightful wrath of his family against Fëanor and set out to rescue his cousin Maedhros. In order to determine the location of the prisoner, Fingon played on his harp and sang. The song rang through the mournful dungeons of Thangorodrim until it was heard and echoed by Maedhros.

On the back of Thorondor, Lord of the Eagles, Fingon rode to Maedhros, but the chain that held his wrist could not be broken. In the end, Maedhros had no recourse but to cut off his own hand as the price of his freedom. Moved by the pity of Fingon, Maedhros repented of his father's evil and passed down the leadership of the Noldor to Fingolfin.

Now Turgon, the second son of Fingolfin, had been living in Nevrast along the western coast of Beleriand, but Ulmo, who ever loved the Elves, appeared to him and bade him leave Nevrast and found a city in the inaccessible mountains near Ered Gorgoroth. Before he left, however, Ulmo instructed Turgon to leave behind him in hiding a sword and a set of armor. One day, a Chosen One would find those tokens and come to rescue Gondolin.

For Gondolin would be the name of the city that Turgon built, a fabled city that would prove to be the final refuge of the Noldor. The Eagles protected its location, preventing the Dragons from flying over it, and not even Morgoth knew the hidden path that led there. In fact, no one who found their way to Gondolin was permitted to leave.

Turgon's sister Aredhel lived with him in Gondolin, but she was surly and rebellious and quickly grew tired of being cooped up in a city isolated from the world. So she left Gondolin and wandered in Beleriand until, in her impulsive folly, she fell in love with a Dark Elf named Eöl. Together they bore Maeglin, a great craftsman, but one who was as prideful as his father and as fiery of soul as Fëanor.

In time, Aredhel wearied of the harshness and cruelty of Eöl, and she fled with Maeglin back to Gondolin—with Eöl in close pursuit. All three were allowed to enter the city, but the gates were closed behind them, and they were forbidden to leave. The proud and sullen Eöl refused to remain as a prisoner and swore he would leave with Maeglin. When his son refused to go, Eöl hurled a spear at him. Moved by love for her son, Aredhel threw herself in front of Maeglin and was mortally wounded by the spear. When she died, the enraged Turgon had Eöl seized, bound, and thrown to his death from a high rock.

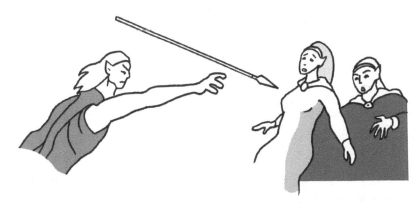

Turgon treated Maeglin kindly, as if he were his own son, but the dark, brooding Maeglin became filled with an unholy lust for Turgon's only child, a lovely Elf maiden named Idril. Idril loved Maeglin as a cousin but was horrified by his forbidden passion for her and rejected all of his advances. And that is how matters remained for many long years to come. Gondolin remained secret and safe, but the seed of evil sown in Maeglin continued to grow until, when it put forth its deadly fruit, it brought ruin to all Beleriand.

For long decades and centuries, battles raged between Morgoth and the Noldor. In one of them, Fingolfin, possessed by the rage of Fëanor, challenged Morgoth to a duel. Morgoth slew Fingolfin, but his foot was severed by Fingolfin's blade and an Eagle marred his face. Never again would he leave his lair. As Morgoth's power receded, that of his lieutenant Sauron increased, and he (Sauron) set out to poison the mind of the Elves.

With the death of his father, Fingon became the next High King of the Noldor. It was about this time that the Edain, the noblest of the Men who had been born under the sun in the east of Middle-earth, moved west to Beleriand and joined the Noldor in their wars against Sauron and Morgoth. But Sauron poisoned their minds as well.

DIGGING DEEPER

Again and again, Tolkien's heroes show pity to the villains in a manner that borders on naiveté. This Christian ethos of turning the other cheek and forgiving one's enemies in hopes that they will reform is extended to Melkor and Sauron in *The Silmarillion* and to Saruman, Wormtongue, and Gollum in *The Lord of the Rings*. In all cases, the villain abuses the pity shown and continues in his treachery. Still, the Catholic Tolkien defends the power of pity, even when the "repentance" of the villain proves to be feigned.

Fëanor is the Achilles of Middle-earth with his honor and courage too often morphing into implacable rage. He is an odd combination of fierce warrior and skilled craftsman, an Elf whose love of battle is tempered by his love of beauty and whose loyalty is as strong as it is destructive. His rash oath and his killing of the Teleri function as a sort of primal sin that runs through several generations of the Noldor, leading, in the end, to their doom.

Of the elder generations of the Noldor, only Galadriel, the daughter of Finarfin, escapes ruin. Tolkien stated that she did not take part in the slaying of the Teleri, though she did choose to leave Valinor, rather than return and beg forgiveness of the Valar. Her story arc is the longest in the legendarium, reaching its climax when she turns down Frodo's offer of the Ring. Galadriel, it was said, had the light of the Two Trees in her hair. It was after she refused to give Fëanor a strand of her golden hair that he forged the Silmarils that caused such death and woe. Later, she would give three strands of her hair to a Dwarf!

Fingon finds the imprisoned Maedhros by the power of song. By the same method, Tolkien will later have Lúthien find her beloved

Beren and faithful Sam find his master Frodo. *The Lord of the Rings* abounds with music and poetry, songs that lift the heart and pierce

through the sorrows of life. The songs are not window dressing; they are essential to the spirit of Tolkien's secondary world.

Alongside the power of song, Tolkien tells a darker theme of maiming. Maedhros loses his hand and Melkor his foot; later, Beren will lose a hand and both Sauron and Frodo a finger. The world is perilous, and most of us do not survive it unscathed. Perhaps Tolkien saw in his mind the terrible wounds and amputations of countless WWI veterans.

The city of Gondolin glimmers with archetypal stories of magical places hiding away from the world: Shangri-La in the snow-capped mountains of Tibet; King Solomon's gold and diamond mines in the fabled land of Ophir; El Dorado and the Fountain of Youth tucked away in some corner of the New World; the walled Garden of Eden itself, now inaccessible to those who long to find the Tree of Life. One thinks too of the lost city of Atlantis, though that ancient kingdom would play a more direct role in the legendarium.

The Silmarillion tells an epic, multi-generational tale that nearly over-whelms its human and elvish characters. And yet, Tolkien manages to weave into his massive tapestry smaller stories like that of Aredhel, Eöl, and Maeglin that attest to his deep humanity and his gift for developing and exploring characters who are tormented and torn apart by misdirected passions and desires.

"And the inner fire of the Silmarils Fëanor made of the blended light of the Trees of Valinor, which lives in them yet, though the Trees have long withered and shine no more. Therefore even in the darkness of the deepest treasury the Silmarils of their own radiance shone like the stars of Varda; and yet, as were they indeed living things, they rejoiced in light and received it and gave it back in hues more marvelous than before" (*The Silmarillion*, chapter seven).

[The curse spoken over the Noldor:] "Tears unnumbered ye shall shed; and the Valar will fence Valinor against you, and shut you out, so that not even the echo of your lamentation shall pass over the mountains. On the House of Fëanor the wrath of the Valar lieth from the West unto the uttermost East, and upon all that will follow them it shall be laid also. Their Oath shall drive them, and yet betray them, and ever snatch away the very treasures that they have sworn to pursue. To evil end shall all things turn that they begin well; and by treason of kin unto kin, and the fear of treason, shall this come to pass. The Dispossessed shall they be for ever" (*The Silmarillion*, chapter nine).

FOUR

The Silmarillion III: Beren and Lúthien

⊙

The Sindar Elf **Thingol** stays behind in Middle-earth.
In Dorlath, he falls in love with the Maia **Melian**.
They have one daughter, **Lúthien**,
Who marries the Man **Beren**, son of **Barahir**.

Galadriel marries **Celeborn** of Doriath.
Their daughter **Celebrían** later marries **Elrond**,
Great-grandson of Beren and Lúthien.

⊙

THE TALE

Although the Noldor and Teleri Elves left Middle-earth for Valinor, there were many others who chose to remain behind. Among them were the Sindar Elves who were as fair as the Noldor were fierce, and whose love of music and of the woods and streams of Middle-earth was as strong as the Noldor's love for gems and for war. They spoke a language called Sindarin that was less lofty than the high elvish Quenya of the Noldor.

The Sindar Elf Thingol had considered leaving for Valinor, but as he passed through the great wood of Doriath, which lay south of Ered Gorgoroth, he met a Maia in bodily form named Melian. He was smitten by her beauty, and the two wed, giving birth to the fairest of the children of Ilúvatar, Lúthien. Melian put a girdle of magic around Doriath to protect it from Morgoth and his allies, and Thingol reigned as High King of Beleriand from his hidden palace of Menegroth, which means "the thousand caves."

When Galadriel, the daughter of Finarfin, came to Beleriand, she met the Sindar Elf Celeborn in Doriath and chose to marry and live with him, rather than with the proud Noldor. They later gave birth to a daughter, Celebrían, but before that time, Galadriel nurtured Lúthien as if she were her own child. She learned too the lore of Melian, and, in the Second and Third Age, she would become a Melian to Lothlórien in Middle-earth.

Now Barahir, who hailed from one of the noblest houses of Men known as the Edain, had fought alongside Men and Elves to defeat the forces of Morgoth. In one battle, he saved the life of Finrod, son of Finarfin and brother of Galadriel and Turgon of Gondolin. Finrod built the great underground fortress of Nargothrond, which lay to the west and slightly to the south of Doriath. For this deed, he was known as Felagund, cave-hewer. He was also a Friend of Men and gave Barahir his ring in gratitude for saving his life.

But Morgoth's generals hunted down Barahir and slew him, leaving his son Beren an orphan with only the ring of Finrod to remember him by. Beren grew up strong and wise, gentle to birds and beasts, but a fierce foe to all the allies of Morgoth. He led a band of outlaws who made raids on Orcs, and won himself legendary status as a Man with the power of an Elf. The fear of death meant nothing to Beren; he feared only bondage.

Sauron, whose power had grown since Morgoth retired to his lair in Thangorodrim, swore that he would capture the outlaw. By guile and treachery, he ambushed Beren's comrades and murdered them in cold blood. Beren alone survived, but was left stranded between Angband to the north and Ered Gorgoroth to the south. Rather than give way to fear, he proceeded to make his way through the Mountains of Terror, a feat that no Man then or since has repeated.

From there he made his way south to Doriath. Though the Girdle of Melian caused trespassers to wander endlessly in a bewildering labyrinth of false turns, Beren penetrated Melian's defenses and found himself in a hidden forest never seen by the eyes of Men. There, in a secluded glade, he gazed upon a sight that changed his life, and the life of Middle-earth, forever. For, as he turned a corner, he came upon Lúthien singing and dancing upon the green grass.

At once, the pain and weariness of all that he had known and suffered melted away. He called out to her, naming her Tinúviel, which means nightingale, but she vanished from his sight, leaving him to wander the cold woods in a daze of longing. But she returned, and her song brought an end to winter. As spring budded across Doriath, the two fell deeply in love, and Lúthien experienced a brief but abiding joy that no Elf has ever known. But their love proved to be as the footsteps of doom to Beleriand.

A bitter and resentful Elf whose love for Lúthien had gone unrequited betrayed her to the suspicious Thingol. Beren was seized and brought before Thingol, who interrogated him severely, accusing him of entering a land forbidden to his race and of stealing the love of his daughter. But Beren answered Thingol that fate had brought him to Doriath and that there he had found something he had not sought but, having found, could not surrender.

Thingol was enraged, but he had made a pledge to Lúthien that he would not harm Beren. Instead, he conceived a plan that would ensure the death of Beren while leaving him innocent of his blood. "You seek my daughter's hand," he said, "and you shall have it. But only if you bring me a gift appropriate for the Princess of Doriath. Bring me a Silmaril from the crown of Morgoth, and you shall have Lúthien for your bride."

Thus Thingol and Beren became snared in the Oath of Fëanor and the Doom of Mandos.

Knowing he could not achieve the task alone, Beren left Doriath and traveled west to Nargothrond, another elvish fortress never before seen by the eyes of Men. There he met Finrod Felagund and showed him the ring he had given to Barahir. In honor of his pledge, Finrod agreed to help Beren, though he feared that when the sons of Fëanor learned of their quest, they would remember their oath and demand the Silmaril for themselves.

And so Finrod left Nargothrond with a troop of Elves, passing his crown to his brother Orodreth. On the way to Thangorodrim, however, they came upon Tol Sirion, the fortress of Sauron. Morgoth's dark lieutenant challenged Finrod to a battle of song. Finrod strove well, but he was vanquished, and his company was imprisoned deep in the earth.

Sauron sent a great wolf to the dungeon to extract confessions from his prisoners as to the nature of their quest, but all refused to speak. One by one the wolf slew the Elves until Finrod and Beren alone were left alive. When the wolf came next for Beren, Finrod unleashed the fullness of his debt to Barahir and gave his life to save that of Beren.

Beren, too, would have been slain in turn had not Lúthien, deep in the forest of Doriath, sensed that the life of her beloved was in danger. She told Thingol that she must go to Beren and help him, but her jealous and suspicious father prevented her from going by imprisoning her in the limbs of a towering tree. But her love for Beren could not be so easily caged. She sang a magic spell that caused her hair to grow to a prodigious length. Of that hair, she made a rope to climb down from the tree and a cloak to enchant her foes.

Freed from Doriath, she fled to Nargothrond, where she was waylaid by Curufin and Celegorm, two of the seven sons of Fëanor. They tried to force her to marry one of them, but she was rescued by Celegorm's noble hound Huan of Valinor, a beast that had been granted the power to understand human speech and to speak thrice in words of his own.

On the back of Huan, Lúthien rode to Tol Sirion where she defeated Sauron in song but allowed him to escape. Then she sang a second song, one that penetrated through the stones and pits of Tol Sirion, uniting her once again with her beloved. Then might the two have lived together in secret happiness, but Beren's promise to Thingol burned within him, and he bade farewell to Lúthien as he set out for Thangorodrim.

It was then that Huan, who had spoken once to Lúthien when he rescued her from his former master, spoke again to tell Beren that his fate and that of Lúthien were intertwined and that they must travel together in search of the Silmaril. Huan used his magic to transform Beren and Lúthien into a wolf and a harpy. In those guises, they made their way deep into the pits of Thangorodrim.

Now Morgoth had known of Sauron's defeat and the quest of Beren, and he had prepared for their coming by taking his hound

Carcharoth, "Red Maw," and feeding it on human flesh. The hound grew to an enormous size so that even the bravest quailed in its presence. It would have prevented the lovers from reaching Morgoth's lair, but Lúthien opened her magic cloak, and her radiant, terrible beauty cast the hound into a deep sleep.

Down, down the endless, winding stairs of Thangorodrim Beren and Lúthien descended until they stood before the throne of Morgoth. On his head rested an iron crown into which he had embedded the three Silmarils he had stolen. As she had done with Sauron, Lúthien strove with Morgoth in song. The contest was fierce, but, in the end, she proved the stronger, casting Morgoth and his court into slumber. Beren leapt forward and, with his knife, pried out one of the Silmarils from the crown.

Even then, all would have been well had not greed seized Beren's heart, making him lust to possess all three Silmarils. He began to pry out the second, but his knife slipped and cut the face of Morgoth. Immediately, Morgoth woke and all Thangorodrim woke with him. To escape, Beren uses the Silmaril to blind the eyes of Carcharoth, but the hound bit off his right hand with which he clutched the Silmaril.

Led by Thorondor, the Eagles rescued Beren and Lúthien, but Carcharoth, the Silmaril burning like fire in his belly, was driven wild with pain and rage. In his fury, he terrorized the countryside of Doriath, so that a party of Elves was formed to run him to ground. During the hunt, Thingol would have been killed by the hound had not Beren leapt in front of him and received the mortal bite of Carcharoth in his flesh. Then only did Thingol see the worth of the man who loved his daughter.

In the end, Huan the hound slew Carcharoth, but it was a victory that cost him his own life. For the third and last time, he spoke, bidding farewell to Beren. Carcharoth's belly was slit open to reveal the clutched right hand of Beren. As soon as it was touched, the hand dissolved, and the Silmaril glowed with the fire of the Trees. Lúthien exerted all her magic to save Beren, but he died in her arms, and his spirit fled to the Halls of Mandos.

Then Lúthien herself descended to the grim Halls of Mandos and sang before him of her love for Beren. Though she moved his iron heart to pity, none of the Valar could grant immortality to Beren, for to do so would be to take from him the gift of Ilúvatar to Men. Instead, Lúthien agreed to surrender her own immortality so that she and Beren could return, briefly, to Middle-earth to live out together a mortal span of years.

Far from Doriath, in the southeast corner of Beleriand, Beren and Lúthien lived in love as man and wife in Tol Galen, the Green Isle. And while they dwelt there together, that place was known as the Land of the Dead that Live. Thus is their song known as the Lay of Leithian, which means Release from Bondage.

DIGGING DEEPER

Throughout Tolkien's legendarium, there run parallel seeds of evil and of good. In *The Silmarillion*, it is the lust for the Silmarils that drives most of the action to its tragic end. In *The Lord of the Rings*, it is the lust for the One Ring that likewise brings death and destruction to so many. (The Arkenstone plays this role in *The Hobbit*, though to a lesser degree.) Against these forces of evil, what hope is there for good?

Enter two seeds of light that offer grace and hope to hold back the corrupting power of the Silmarils, Arkenstone, and Ring. The first, as we will see in later chapters, is the Two Trees. Though they are destroyed by Melkor and Ungoliant, a sapling from the Trees finds its way to the island of Númenor, and, from there, to Middle-earth, where it springs up as the White Tree of Gondor.

Thus are the Two Trees linked themselves to the second seed, the sacred bloodline that finds its culmination in Aragorn, the Messianic King of Gondor, and Arwen, the granddaughter of Galadriel. This royal bloodline begins with the marriage of Thingol the Elf and Melian the Maia and continues with the marriage of Beren the Man and Lúthien the Elf. The continuation of that bloodline will be traced in the chapters that follow.

In one sense, all the events of *The Silmarillion* and *Lord of the Rings*, even the bad ones, work together to preserve that bloodline, as they do in the Old Testament. For Jesus the Messiah to be born in the fullness of time, many strange, unexpected things must occur. Consider what must happen in the Old Testament to preserve the bloodline of Christ:

- Isaac is miraculously born to Sarah, who is well past childbearing years.
- Jacob steals the birthright and blessing from his older brother.
- Judah is the son of Jacob and a woman (Leah) he was tricked into marrying.
- Tamar tricks her father-in-law Judah into fathering a child with her.
- Rahab, a pagan harlot, is accepted into Israel and the sacred bloodline.
- Ruth, a foreigner, loses her Jewish husband but is redeemed by another.
- David's adulterous affair with Bathsheba leads to Solomon's birth.
- Mary, though a virgin, gives birth to Jesus.

In *The Da Vinci Code*, Dan Brown popularized a longstanding conspiracy theory that Jesus and Mary Magdalene fathered a secret bloodline that was guarded by the Knights Templar in the coded formula of the Holy Grail (if one letter is shifted, San Graal becomes Sang Raal, "royal blood"). And yet, ironically, the real secret bloodline is the one that runs, circuitously, from Abraham to Christ. This Tolkien surely saw, for the line he traces from Thingol and Melian to Aragorn and Arwen is equally circuitous.

At one exciting point in the legendarium, the Silmarils, Trees, and sacred bloodline all join together. As we will see in chapter six, the last of the Silmarils, which held within it the last pure light from the Two Trees, became the Star of Eärendil, grandson of Beren and Lúthien and grandfather of Arwen.

The story of Beren and Lúthien is perhaps the most tender and beautiful in the entire legendarium. It is made even more memorable by its use of three archetypes common to myths and legends. Beren is the blue-blooded orphan whose true worth is revealed when he faces a challenge that allows him to fulfill his destiny. Other such orphans include Perseus, Theseus, and Hercules; Romulus, Moses, and Cyrus; Mowgli, Tarzan, and Pecos Bill; Arthur, Percival, and Siegfried; Oliver Twist, Luke Skywalker, and Harry Potter.

The love between Beren and Lúthien is that of any number of star-crossed lovers from Tristan and Isolde to Romeo and Juliet, Orpheus and Eurydice to Cathy and Heathcliff. The impossible task Beren must go on to win the prize he seeks is itself a recurring theme, most famously realized in Jason's quest for the Golden Fleece and Perseus' quest to cut off the head of Medusa, quests that won them the love of Medea and Andromeda.

For Tolkien, however, these archetypes, as we saw in chapter one, had a deeply personal meaning that linked Beren's love for Lúthien to his own love for Edith. So deep was that connection that, shortly after Edith died, Tolkien wrote a letter to his son Michael that expressed his love and regret for Edith in terms of the sad tale of Beren and Lúthien.

I met the Lúthien Tinúviel of my own personal "romance" with her long dark hair, fair face and starry eyes, and beautiful voice. . . . But now she has gone before Beren, leaving him indeed one-handed, but he has no power to move the inexorable Mandos, and there is no . . . Land of the Dead that Live, in this Fallen Kingdom of Arda, where the servants of Morgoth are worshipped.

"It is told in the Lay of Leithian that Beren came stumbling into Doriath grey and bowed as with many years of woe, so great had been the torment of the road. But wandering in the summer in the woods of Neldoreth he came upon Lúthien, daughter of Thingol and Melian, at a time of evening under moonrise, as she danced upon the unfading grass in the glades beside Esgalduin. Then all memory of his pain departed from him, and he fell into an enchantment; for Lúthien was the most beautiful of all the Children of Ilúvatar. Blue was her raiment as the unclouded heaven, but her eyes were grey as the starlit evening; her mantle was sewn with golden flowers, but her hair was dark as the shadows of twilight. As the light upon the leaves of trees, as the voice of clear waters, as the stars above the mists of the world, such was her glory and her loveliness; and in her face was a shining light" (*The Silmarillion*, chapter nineteen).

[Beren's words to Thingol:] "My fate, O King, led me hither, through perils such as few even of the Elves would dare. And here I have found what I sought not indeed, but finding I would possess for ever. For it is above all gold and silver, and beyond all jewels. Neither rock, nor steel, nor the fires of Morgoth, nor all the powers of the Elf-kingdoms, shall keep from me the treasure that I desire. For Lúthien your daughter is the fairest of all the Children of the World" (*The Silmarillion*, chapter nineteen).

FIVE

The Silmarillion IV: The Children of Húrin

❂

Húrin of the Edain and **Morwen** bear
Túrin, later called **Turambar**, and
Nienor, later called **Níniel**.
Finduilas, daughter of **Orodreth**, loves Túrin.

❂

THE TALE

As the alliance between Men and Elves grew stronger, Morgoth feared that, if united, they would breach his fortress of Thangorodrim. To disrupt their unity, he used lies and deceit to drive a wedge between the Children of Ilúvatar. Soon thereafter, Fingon and his army, supported by unlooked-for aid from Gondolin, advanced to the very gates of Angband. On that day, they would have overthrown Morgoth had not the treachery of Men prevented their victory and led to the slaying of Fingon by a Balrog.

Thus did Fingon's kingdom and fortress of Hithlum, which had long stood as a bastion of safety just west of Angband, fall to the enemy. Morgoth repopulated Hithlum with Men he had corrupted, and Turgon of Gondolin became High King of the Noldor.

Now, in an earlier battle, Húrin and Huor, brothers of the Edain, had been trapped by the enemy in Angband. But Thorondor and his Eagles had rescued them from the battlefield and flown them to Gondolin, the first Men to see that hidden kingdom and be permitted to leave again with their lives. Alas, in the fateful battle where Fingon fell,

Húrin was captured by Morgoth and chained to a chair high on the ramparts of Thangorodrim.

Fiercely did the enemy question Húrin as to the location of Gondolin, but he would not speak. And so, to break the proud spirit of Húrin, Morgoth left him there to watch helplessly as his family was destroyed from without and within. At the time, Húrin's wife Morwen, their young son Túrin, and daughter Nienor lived in Hithlum. Fearing for her son's safety, Morwen sent her son to Doriath to be raised by Thingol.

Thingol loved the boy as he had Lúthien, but Túrin, through no fault of his own, won the envy of Saeros the Elf. Though Saeros taunted him, Túrin bore it with patience; he even showed mercy after defeating Saeros in a fight that Saeros had initiated. One day, while chasing Túrin through the woods, Saeros tripped on a stone near the cliff's edge and fell to his death. Fearing Thingol's wrath, and too proud to stand for judgment, Túrin fled Doriath.

Then did Túrin, the only Man beside Beren to see Doriath,

69

become, like Beren, the leader of an outlaw band. He sought always to instill justice in his companions, even putting one to death who had tried to rape a girl. Yet he was a wild and unkempt man, rash and impulsive. Though noble, he had few friends, laughed seldom, and was never merry.

Thingol pined for Túrin and sent Beleg the Elf to return him to Doriath that they might be reconciled and live as before. To assist Beleg in his search, Melian provided him with lembas, the waybread of the Elves. This was the first time lembas had been shared with the sons of Men; it would not happen again until the end of the Third Age when Galadriel shared it with the Fellowship in their quest to destroy the Ring of Sauron.

But Túrin could no more forgive himself than he could accept the pity of others. Rather than return to Doriath, Beleg chose to join Túrin. Even when Túrin's band accidentally killed the son of a Petty-dwarf named Mîm, and Túrin, out of compassion, chose to stay with and protect Mîm, Beleg remained. This, despite the fact that the Petty-Dwarves hated the Noldor, for they, who had built Nargothrond, saw the Noldor as invaders.

At this time, Morgoth, who hated Túrin as he had Beren, had sent out Orcs to capture him. When, instead, they captured Mîm, the Petty-dwarf betrayed Túrin, whom the Orcs seized and tied to a post. That night, Beleg infiltrated the enemy camp to rescue Túrin. Alas, as he cut Túrin's bonds, Beleg's sword slipped and cut the foot of Túrin. The sleeping Túrin woke with a start, and, in his confusion, seized the sword and killed Beleg.

Mourning bitterly, Túrin wandered in Beleriand until he came, as Beren had before him, to Nargothrond. Though he came as a prisoner under a false name, his courage quickly won over the Elves. Finduilas, daughter of Orodreth the king, fell deeply in love with him, provoking the jealousy of the Elf Gwindor. When Gwindor could not convince her to renounce her fatal love for a mortal Man, he revealed the true identity of Túrin.

Túrin was angered by this, but Orodreth embraced him as a great hero. Eager for revenge against Morgoth, Túrin convinced Orodreth to build a bridge over the River Narog so that he could march his troops out of the city. The deed was a rash and foolish one, for it allowed the troops of Morgoth to attack the city that had long been protected by the river.

Led by the fierce Dragon Glaurung, Morgoth's armies laid waste to Nargothrond and slew Orodreth and Gwindor. As he lay dying, Gwindor begged Túrin to rescue Finduilas, but he arrived too late to save her. For he was delayed by Glaurung, whose lidless eyes cast a spell upon Túrin. As he stood, frozen by the hypnotic stare of the Dragon, Glaurung taunted Túrin with his crimes: "thankless fosterling, outlaw, slayer of thy friend, thief of love, usurper of Nargothrond, captain foolhardy, and deserter of thy kind."

It was then that Túrin realized, to his shame, that he had cursed and destroyed everything he had touched and everyone he had loved. Horrified by the reflection shown him by the Dragon, he fled, changed his name to Turambar, and lived as a wildman of the woods.

Sometime before this, Túrin's mother Morwen and sister Nienor had left Hithlum and journeyed to Doriath. Thingol and Melian told them what had happened and begged them to remain in Doriath where they could be protected. But they were stubborn and proud and refused the good advice that had been given them.

As they sought Túrin in the wilds of Beleriand, Glaurung ambushed and bewitched them, causing them to forget themselves. Morwen receded into the woods and was lost, while Nienor fled, naked, in terror. As he knelt in sorrow before the tomb of Finduilas, Túrin turned and saw the naked body of Nienor asleep on the grass. Not recognizing the sister he had not seen since she was a child, Túrin called her Níniel; then, taking it as a sign that he should meet her beside the tomb of the Elf maiden he had destroyed, he married her.

Their love was real and Níniel became pregnant with the child of Turambar, but they could not escape the dark fate brought on by their forbidden marriage. Glaurung returned and strove with Túrin in a final showdown of rage and fire. Túrin defeated his enemy, but was deeply wounded. Nienor found him and tended to his wounds, but, even as she did, the Dragon woke and, with its final breath, revealed to her the bitter truth of her love.

In anguish and despair, Nienor leapt to her death from the cliff. Sometime later, when Túrin recovered from his wound, he was met by Brandir, a man who had loved Nienor in the same way that Gwindor had loved Finduilas. Bitter at Túrin, Brandir told him the truth of all that had occurred, only to be slain by Túrin in a fit of rage. Later, however, Túrin learned that Brandir had spoken truly. It was then that he took Beleg's sword in hand, the very sword by which he had slain his friend, and drove it into his own chest.

All these things Húrin saw from the chair to which Morgoth had bound him, though the enemy only let him see what he knew would provoke the maximum degree of despair. It was only then that Morgoth released him to wander back into Beleriand. As he made his way south, he passed by the mountains where Gondolin lay. Knowing the city was there, though ignorant of its exact location, Húrin called out to Turgon for aid. None came, but now Morgoth knew Gondolin lay closer than he thought to Angband and Ered Gorgoroth.

Húrin made his way to the ruins of Nargothrond where he discovered Mîm plundering the treasures that had been left behind. Húrin killed Mîm who had caused such harm to Túrin and took for himself the priceless necklace of the Dwarves. He traveled next to Doriath, where he gave the necklace to Thingol but then shamed and blamed him for failing to care for the boy that had been entrusted to him. To help Húrin understand that her husband was blameless, Melian revealed to him the truth of all that had passed.

During his journey to Nargothrond, Húrin had come upon Morwen, who had remembered herself again but who had died the following day from the grief that lay heavy upon her. Now that he had learned the fullness of truth from Melian, Húrin gave way fully to grief and cast himself into the sea. Thus did the malice of Morgoth bear its full and bitter fruit.

DIGGING DEEPER

The tale of Túrin Turambar is the longest and most tragic of all the tales told in *The Silmarillion*, a tale that reflects *Oedipus* and other Greek tragedies in its piling up of taboo crimes within the relations of a single family. Just as Oedipus does not knowingly kill his father or marry his mother, so Túrin commits most of his destructive deeds accidentally or in ignorance. Nevertheless, the deeds bring with them a ritual guilt that demands expiation.

The tale possesses a primitive and primal power that traps the reader in a kind of nightmare, one in which the revelation of truth at the end brings darkness rather than illumination, destruction rather than hope. Túrin is trapped in a net of fate; the more he attempts to claw his way out, the more he becomes enmeshed in the trap. In the tale, love leads to betrayal or heartache or sin, rarely to joy, freedom, and release from bondage.

As in the tale of Beren and Lúthien, archetypes abound, but they tend to be darker, shot through with savage irony and a deep pessimism and fatalism. To increase the hopelessness of it all, Tolkien presents it as if it were a film being watched by Húrin from his seat atop Thangorodrim: a captive audience if there ever was one! Just as, in *The Lord of the Rings*, Sauron will cause Denethor to despair by showing him, through the palantír, only what he wants him to see, so Morgoth carefully manipulates what Húrin sees in order to break his spirit and turn him into a tool for bringing about the ruin of Beleriand.

Denethor has something else in common with the tragic trio of Túrin, Húrin, and Nienor. All four die as suicides, something that is very rare in Tolkien's legendarium. In Catholic thought, suicide is a grave sin, not only because it robs God of his prerogatives as the giver and taker of life, but because it is an act motivated by pride and despair. All four, though less so Nienor, possess a fierce stubbornness that feeds and is fed by their despair.

Still, even here, Tolkien does not give way to cynicism, skepticism, or misanthropy. The reader finds enlightenment, even as he does in *Oedipus*. Through the sorrow and death of Túrin's tale a greater purpose is worked out, one that eludes the schemes of Morgoth.

> ". . . and straightaway [Túrin] fell under the binding spell of the lidless eyes of the dragon, and was halted moveless. Then for a long time he stood as one graven of stone; and they two were alone, silent before the doors of Nargothrond. But Glaurung spoke again, taunting Túrin, and he said: "Evil have been all thy ways, son of Húrin. Thankless fosterling, outlaw, slayer of thy friend, thief of love, usurper of Nargothrond, captain foolhardy, and deserter of thy kin. As thralls thy mother and thy sister live in Dor-lómin, in misery and want. Thou art arrayed as a prince, but they go in rags; and for thee they yearn, but thou carest not for that. Glad may thy father be to learn that he hath such a son; as learn he shall." And Túrin being

under the spell of Glaurung hearkened to his words, and he saw himself as in a mirror misshapen by malice, and loathed that which he saw" (*The Silmarillion*, chapter twenty-one).

"And at the last Melian spoke, and said: "Húrin Thalion, Morgoth hath bewitched thee; for he that seeth through Morgoth's eyes, willing or unwilling, seeth all things crooked. Long was Túrin thy son fostered in the halls of Menegroth, and shown love and honour as the son of the King; and it was not by the King's will nor by mine that he came never back to Doriath. And afterwards thy wife and thy daughter were harboured here with honour and goodwill; and we sought by all means that we might to dissuade Morwen from the road to Nargothrond. With the voice of Morgoth thou dost now upbraid thy friends" (*The Silmarillion*, chapter twenty-two).

SIX

The Silmarillion V: The Fall of Beleriand

❂

Huor, brother of Húrin, is the father of Tuor.
Tuor marries Idril, daughter of Turgon of Gondolin;
Their son, Eärendil, marries Elwing,
Who is the daughter of Nimloth and Dior,
Who is the son of Beren and Lúthien.

❂

THE TALE

When Húrin presented Thingol with the necklace of the Dwarves, he aroused in him the lust of the Silmarils that had been slowly poisoning his soul. Determined to possess the most costly jewel in all of Middle-earth, he ordered a group of Dwarves to take the Silmaril and embed it within the necklace that they had made for Finrod and which they called the Nauglamir. The result combined the skill and beauty of the Dwarves and the Elves and was altogether precious and desirable.

So desirable, in fact, that the Dwarves who fashioned it lusted for it and demanded it of Thingol. When Thingol refused to give them the Nauglamir, they fell upon him, slew him, and fled to the east with their stolen prize. But they did not make it far before they were caught and killed and the Nauglamir given to Melian. But the necklace, beautiful as it was, brought no joy to Melian who sat long in sorrow by the body of Thingol.

She knew that doom lay heavy upon Doriath, but her sadness was too great to prevent it. As she wept and grieved, the Girdle she had wrapped around Doriath collapsed, and she herself vanished from Middle-earth, never to be seen again. Soon after, a group of Dwarves from the east, hearing of their murdered brothers, raided Doriath and sacked Menegroth. It was here that the enmity between Elf and Dwarf began.

Seizing the Nauglamir for themselves, the Dwarves headed east, but fate put them in the path of Beren, who had journeyed north from Tol Galen. Beren slew the evil Dwarves and brought the necklace with him back to the Green Isle. Years before, Beren and Lúthien had born a single son, Dior, an immortal Elf in whose veins ran the blood of Man and of Elf as well as the spirit of Melian the Maia. When he came of age, Dior journeyed to Doriath where, as Thingol's heir, he ruled with Nimloth his queen.

Meanwhile, Lúthien wore the Nauglamir that Beren had brought her. As long as the Silmaril shone upon her breast, Tol Galen became like another Valinor, but the beauty of the gem, which was never meant for our mortal world, consumed the life of Lúthien and hastened her death. When she died, the necklace was sent to Doriath and was placed around the neck of Dior. Then Beren and Lúthien together vanished from Beleriand.

As long as Lúthien wore the Silmaril, the sons of Fëanor did not dare to attack her, but when it passed to Dior, they remembered the dreadful oath they had taken and attacked Doriath. Sadly, what neither Morgoth nor the Dwarves could destroy was destroyed by the Elves themselves. This was the second kin-slaying of the Elves; it claimed the lives of Dior, Nimloth, and their two sons, together with three of the seven sons of Fëanor.

All hope, however, was not lost. Dior's daughter Elwing escaped the fall of Doriath and fled, with the Nauglamir, down the River Sirion to its southernmost port. There, at the mouths of the Sirion, she waited with the survivors for the last hand of fate to be played.

With the fall of Doriath, all the camps and fortresses of the Elves were gone save one. As Ulmo had prophesied long ago, Gondolin was now the last hope of Beleriand.

Now Húrin's brother Huor had a son named Tuor, and he felt com-pelled to visit the seaport of Nevrast, where Turgon once had lived. There, by the shore of the sea, Ulmo appeared

to the mortal Tuor and revealed to him the sword and the armor that Turgon had hidden there to be found, in the fullness of time, by a Chosen One. Then, as if he walked in a trance, Tuor was led by Ulmo to seek and find the hidden city of Gondolin.

Turgon remembered the visit of Húrin and Huor and accepted with joy the arrival of the latter's son. Tuor warned Turgon, in the words taught him by Ulmo, to leave Gondolin and flee to Sirion, but Turgon, proud of the beauty and unconquerable strength of his city, refused to heed. In that decision, he was led astray by Maeglin, who yet lusted for Idril.

As Lúthien had fallen in love with the mortal Beren and Finduilas with Túrin, so Idril fell for Tuor, filling Maeglin with a cancerous envy. For seven years, Tuor remained in Gondolin, enthralled by its beauty and its wisdom. At the end of that time, Turgon consented, and Tuor and Idril were wed, the second union of Man and Elf.

Sometime later, while wandering outside Gondolin, Maeglin was captured by Morgoth's men who had been patrolling the hills ever since Húrin had revealed the region where the city was hidden. It was then that the evil seed planted by Aredhel's hasty marriage to Eöl bore its bitter fruit. In return for being named Lord of Gondolin, under the vassalage of Morgoth, and given Idril as his bride, Maeglin agreed to betray the city. This was the worst betrayal of the First Age and the chief cause of the Fall of Gondolin.

As the forces of Morgoth began to sack the city, Maeglin, driven by his lust, attempted to seize Idril. But Tuor grabbed the villain, held him aloft, and threw him from the cliff to his death. So did the traitor die in the same manner as his treacherous father. As his beloved city crumbled about him, Turgon too was slain, and Gil-Galad, the son of his brother Fingon, became the last High King of the Noldor to rule in Middle-earth.

81

But Tuor and Idril, with their son Eärendil, escaped down the Great River and joined the remnant of the Elves at the mouths of the Sirion. When they had grown older, Tuor and Idril set off together on a boat in search of Valinor. Though they were never seen again, it is said that they reached the far west, and that Tuor was granted a fate like no other mortal; for he was joined forever with the Noldor whom he loved.

Ulmo pleaded long and hard with Manwë to forgive the Noldor and come to their aid, but he was not moved. For that, a different advocate would be needed.

Drawn together by fate, Eärendil and Elwing were joined in marriage, thus uniting the mixed blood of Tuor and Idril and Beren and Lúthien. Shortly after, Eärendil left Elwing behind and sailed west for Valinor. He did so for two reasons: to find the ship of his parents, and to beg the Valar to come to their aid. Though he failed in the first, he did, against all odds, find his way to Valinor.

The reason he was able to do so is linked to one of the saddest events in the history of Beleriand. When the remaining four sons of Fëanor learned that the Silmaril was held by Elwing at the mouths of Sirion, they attacked and slew many innocent Elves. This was the third and last kin-slaying of the Elves, a slaying that also claimed the lives of two of Fëanor's sons. But Elwing escaped with the Nauglamir. To assist her in her flight, Ulmo transformed her into a bird. In that form, she flew to Eärendil and gave him the necklace.

It was the light from the Silmaril, which increased in brightness as he neared the Undying Lands, that led Eärendil to Valinor and allowed him to present his plea directly to the Valar.

Manwë consented, but decreed that Eärendil and Elwing must never again set foot in Middle-earth. To Eärendil, however, they gave a star-boat named Vingilot with which he sailed across the sky. To those who lived in Middle-earth, his boat was the morning and the evening star, and the light from that star was the light of the Silmaril.

As they had promised, the Valar came, and, in an alliance with Elves and Men, fought an apocalyptic battle that defeated Morgoth but laid waste to Beleriand. They then seized Morgoth and thrust him outside the world where he could no longer harm the peoples of Middle-earth. But the evil he had planted remained to flower in the schemes of Sauron.

As for the other two Silmarils, they were stolen by Maedhros and Maglor, the remaining two sons of Fëanor. The Valar gave each of them a chance to return what he had stolen, but each refused. It was then that the Silmarils began to burn them terribly, until, to free themselves from the pain, the first cast himself into a volcano and the second into the sea. So did the three Silmarils come to rest in water, in air, and in the fiery earth.

DIGGING DEEPER

One of the running themes in the Old Testament is that God always preserves a remnant of the faithful to carry on his plans for human history. Thus, after the prophet Isaiah asks Yahweh how long he will continue to punish his people with destruction and exile, God answers with a promise that, though the punishment will be severe, a tenth shall remain:

> "Until the cities are laid waste and without inhabitant,
> The houses are without a man,
> The land is utterly desolate,
> The Lord has removed men far away,
> And the forsaken places are many in the midst of the land.
> But yet a tenth will be in it,
> And will return and be for consuming,
> As a terebinth tree or as an oak,

Whose stump remains when it is cut down.
So the holy seed shall be its stump" (Isaiah 6:11-13; NKJV).

Notice here that there will be a tenth out of the tenth, a remnant out of the remnant. The winnowing will be fierce, but the holy seed shall endure.

In Tolkien's account of the sacred bloodline that connects Beren and Lúthien to Aragorn and Arwen, he emphasized how many times that messianic line came close to being wiped out. Again and again, a single child survives the fall of Gondolin or the kin-slayings at Doriath and the mouths of Sirion to perpetuate the royal line.

In book one, chapter eleven of *The Lord of the Rings*, Aragorn shares with the Hobbits the tragic love story of Beren and Lúthien and their quest for the Silmaril. His telling is too long to quote here, but he climaxes it by highlighting the sacred line that began with the Elf Maiden who gave up her immortality for love:

"There live still those of whom Lúthien was the foremother, and it is said that her line shall never fail. Elrond of Rivendell is of that Kin. For of Beren and Lúthien was born Dior Thingol's heir; and of him Elwing the White whom Eärendil wedded, he that sailed his ship out of the mists of the world into the seas of heaven with the Silmaril upon his brow. And of Eärendil came the Kings of Númenor, that is Westernesse."

At this point, Aragorn does not reveal that he is the last surviving heir of the Kings of Númenor or that his beloved, the Elf Maiden Arwen, is the daughter of Elrond.

As for Eärendil and his magic star-boat, that strange and beautiful tale provided the subject matter for twenty-two-year-old Tolkien's first poem about Middle-earth. For Tolkien, Eärendil was Venus, both Lucifer (the morning star) and Hesperus (the evening star), and a harbinger of good in the heavens. That star, which preserved the light of the Silmaril, and thus of the Trees, would go on to play a key role in *The Lord of the Rings*.

One night as Eärendil flew over Middle-earth, Galadriel gathered the light from the star into her Mirror and preserved it in the Phial she later gave to Frodo—the very Phial Frodo and Sam used to defeat the spider Shelob, last descendant of Ungoliant, destroyer of the Two Trees. Later, as he lay shivering in the desolate wastes of Mordor, Sam looked up at the White Star of Eärendil, and it gave him hope to finish the journey. It proved to be, like Galadriel's Phial, a light in dark places when all other lights had gone out.

The stories from *The Silmarillion* form the background to the War of the Ring, which brought an end to the Third Age of Middle-earth, as the defeat of Morgoth did the First Age. Those stories also appear in *The Hobbit*, but in a more subtle and elusive manner. Here, from chapter eight of *The Hobbit*, is Tolkien's simplified telling of how the enmity between the Elves and the Dwarves began. I will make the links to *The Silmarillion* in brackets:

"In ancient days they [the Sindar Elves] had had wars with some of the Dwarves, whom they accused of stealing their treasure [the Nauglamir]. It is only fair to say that the Dwarves gave a different account, and said that they only took what was their due, for the elf-king [Thingol] had bargained with them to shape his raw gold and silver [putting the Silmaril in the Nauglamir], and had afterwards refused to give them their pay. If the elf-king had a weakness it was for treasure, especially for silver and white gems; and though his hoard was rich, he was ever eager for more, since he had not yet as great a treasure as other elf-lords [the Noldor] of old. His people [the Sindar] neither mined nor worked metals or jewels, nor did they bother much with trade or with tilling the earth."

". . . it is said and sung that Lúthien wearing that necklace and that immortal jewel was the vision of greatest beauty and glory that has ever been outside the realm of Valinor; and for a little while the Land of the Dead that Live became like a vision of the land of the Valar, and no place has been since so fair, so fruitful, or so filled with light" (*The Silmarillion*, chapter twenty-two).

"But Morgoth himself the Valar thrust through the Door of Night beyond the Walls of the World, into the Timeless Void; and a guard is set for ever on those walls, and Eärendil keeps watch upon the ramparts of the sky. Yet the lies that Melkor, the mighty and accursed, Morgoth Bauglir, the Power of Terror and of Hate, sowed in the hearts of Elves and Men are a seed that does not die and cannot be destroyed; and ever and anon it sprouts anew, and will bear dark fruit even unto the latest days" (*The Silmarillion*, chapter twenty-four).

SEVEN

The Silmarillion VI: The Second Age

Eärendil is the father of **Elrond** and **Elros**.
Elros chooses mortality and fathers the Kings of Númenor.
The last of these, **Aragorn**, marries **Arwen**,
Daughter of Elrond and **Celebrían**, daughter of **Galadriel**.

Elendil, with his sons **Isildur** and **Anárion**, flee Númenor
   before it falls.
Elendil establishes the **Kingdom of Arnor** in the North;
His sons establish the **Kingdom of Gondor** in the South.
Isildur rules from **Minas Ithil**, Tower of the Moon;
Anárion rules from **Minas Anor**, Tower of the Sun.
Osgiliath is built in the River **Anduin**;
Isengard and **Orthanc** are built at the foot of the Misty
   Mountains.

THE TALE

With the defeat of Morgoth, the First Age of Middle-earth came to a close. (Just so, the Second and Third Ages would each end with a victory over Sauron.) In that defeat, Elves and Men played a key role, and the Valar rewarded the Elves by inviting them to return to Valinor. Those that remained behind—chief among them, Galadriel and Celeborn, Gil-Galad, and Círdan the Shipwright—were told they could, when ready, board a ship and sail for the west. All but Arwen chose to do so at the end of the Third Age.

To Elrond and Elros, the sons of Eärendil, the Valar granted a great boon. They could choose whether they would remain an Elf or join with the race of Men. Elrond chose immortality and fathered Arwen, the fairest Elf Maiden since Lúthien. Elros, like his great-grandmother Lúthien, chose mortality.

As for the Dúnedain, the Edain of the west who fought Morgoth, the Valar gave to them the star-shaped island of Númenor, or Westernesse, that stood in the vast ocean between Middle-earth to the east and Valinor to the west. For their king, he gave them Elros and his descendants, and to them all he granted a span of life three times that of normal Men.

Though they, like Eärendil, were great shipbuilders and navigators, they were forbidden to sail to the Undying Lands of Valinor lest they lust for immortality and so forsake the gift of Ilúvatar to Men. They could, however, when the sky was clear, catch a glimpse of Tol Eressëa, from which island the Elves of the west would sail to visit them.

This was the Golden Age of Men, when the Dúnedain sailed their ships to Middle-earth and took pity on the lesser Men who lived there, enslaved as they were to Sauron and to their own lust and ignorance. These Men they tutored, doing all they could to raise them out of their primitive state. But they established no colonies in Middle-earth, for their motives were pure. In those days, they were looked upon as gods and great sea-kings.

But as the centuries rolled by, discontent rose, and many of the Dúnedain hated Elros for choosing mortality. To make up for the immortality they felt had been stolen from them, they built monuments to themselves and their dead and mined precious gems. To expand their wealth, they built colonies on Middle-earth and exploited the labor of Men.

Now Sauron had entrenched himself in the southeast corner of Middle-earth, in the land of Mordor. Around the year 1500 of the Second Age, Sauron helped Celebrimbor, son of Curufin and grandson of Fëanor, to construct a series of rings. Then, in the depths of Mount Doom, Sauron secretly forged One Ring with the power to rule all the others. Seven of those rings he gave to the Dwarves and nine to Men, but the three that had been forged by Celebrimbor alone he could not take. These had the power to hold back decay.

One ring to rule them all.

The moment Sauron put on the One Ring, Celebrimbor sensed that he had been betrayed and hid away the three rings. After Sauron slew Celebrimbor, they were entrusted to Galadriel, Gil-Galad, who gave his ring to Elrond, and Círdan, who gave his to Gandalf. Meanwhile, Sauron sought to conquer the north of Middle-earth but was prevented, and driven back to Mordor, by a fleet of warships from Númenor.

Still, though the Dúnedain saved Middle-earth from being overrun by Sauron, their moral decline continued unabated. Their twenty-fourth and final king, Ar-Pharazôn, decided in his pride that if he could not go to Valinor, he would make himself absolute ruler of Middle-earth. Knowing he could not defeat Ar-Pharazôn, Sauron allowed himself to be defeated, captured, and brought back to Númenor as a captive.

Once there, he played the role of Counselor and Friend of Man. But he used his position to sow discontent between Men and Elves and to convince the Dúnedain that Melkor, not Ilúvatar, was the highest god. He increased, as well, their obsessive fear of death, so that, in the end, they embarked on a fatal and disastrous campaign against Valinor itself.

Though they landed on the Undying Lands, they did not see the Valar. Rather, they were slain for their sacrilege, and Ilúvatar, in his wrath, sent a wave to destroy Númenor and bury her beneath the sea. Along with Númenor, all of Beleriand was covered by the flood, leaving only the lands of Middle-earth as they stood in the Third Age. Then was the shape of the world changed from a flat disk to a round globe, and the Straight Road by which a ship could sail from Middle-earth to Valinor was hidden from Men.

The name of Númenor, too, was changed to Akallabêth, the Downfallen, or, as it is called in the tongue of the Sindar, Atalantë. As for Sauron, he too was destroyed in the wave, and though his evil spirit endured, he could never again take on a pleasing form by which to fool his enemies and masquerade as a Maia of light.

But not all the Dúnedain perished in the great wave. While the King's Men carried out the evil orders of Ar-Pharazôn, a group of Men known as the Faithful stayed true to the Valar, the Elves, and Ilúvatar. Their leader, Amandil, had tried, like Eärendil before him, to reach Valinor and warn the Valar, but he was never heard from again. But his son Elendil survived, and he fled Númenor with his sons Isildur and Anárion.

They brought with them the palantíri, the seven Seeing Stones that had been forged in Valinor by Fëanor and that had the power to see things from afar. They brought as well a sapling from the sacred Tree of Númenor, which had itself been grown from a sapling from the Two Trees of Valinor. Sauron had ordered the Tree of Númenor to be destroyed, but Isildur stole into his camp and rescued a sapling before the Tree was burned. From that sapling grew the White Tree of Gondor that was restored at the crowning of Aragorn.

In Middle-earth, Elendil set up the Kingdom of Arnor in the north, while his sons established the Kingdom of Gondor in the south. In the center of the great River Anduin that separates the White Mountains from Mordor, they built the fortress of Osgiliath. They then built, on the Mordor side of the river, Minas Ithil (the Tower of the Moon from which Isildur reigned) and, on the other, Minas Anor (the Tower of the Sun from which Anárion reigned). Northwest of Gondor at the base of the Misty Mountains, they built the Ring of Isengard and, in its center, the Tower of Orthanc.

At these four sites, they housed four of the palantíri. The other three were housed in Arnor, with the central stone at the watchtower of Weathertop. By means of the seven Stones, the Realms in Exile communicated with each other and kept watch on Sauron.

Though the seven rings of the Dwarves drove them underground in search of wealth and the three rings of the Elves seduced them into holding Middle-earth in perpetual stasis, neither Dwarf nor Elf ever followed Sauron. Not so the Men to whom the nine rings were given. Sauron corrupted them, and they faded into Nazgûl, Ring-wraiths who serve and worship the Ring and its Dark Lord.

As Sauron's power in Mordor grew, a new alliance was formed between Men and Elves to defend Middle-earth. The armies of Arnor and Gondor gathered in a hidden valley by the northwest slope of the Misty Mountains called Rivendell, home and shelter of Elrond and his Elves. Together, they mounted an assault on Dagorlad, north of the Black Gate that led into Mordor. The Men of Dunharrow had sworn to Isildur that they would fight by his side, but they were corrupted by Sauron and broke their sacred oath.

The forces of Elrond and Elendil won the day, but so fierce was the battle and so high the casualties that the ground was laid waste and decayed into rotting marshes filled forever with the bodies of the dead. The Elves and Men who survived laid siege to Mordor and succeeded in drawing Sauron out of his Dark Tower. In the battle that ensued, Gil-Galad, Elendil, and Anárion were all slain, and Narsil, the blade of Elendil, was shattered.

It was in that moment of certain defeat that Isildur took up the shards of Narsil and cut the Ring from the finger of Sauron. The Dark Lord fell into darkness and would have ceased to exist had not the wisdom of Men failed. Elrond and Círdan, knowing that Sauron's life was tied to the Ring, led Isildur to the heart of Mount Doom and bade him cast the Ring into the fire in which it had been formed. Thus only could the Ring be unmade. But he refused, like Fëanor before him, to surrender so precious a prize.

Isildur slipped the Ring on his finger

and, rendered invisible by its magic, stole away. Later, as he marched along the River Anduin to be reunited with his family in Arnor, he was waylaid by a party of Orcs. He put on the Ring and leapt, invisible, into the Anduin. But the Ring betrayed him, slipping from his finger and settling in the murky bottom of the river. Now visible, Isildur was pierced with Orc arrows and breathed his last.

Thus ended the Second Age of Middle-earth and the last alliance of Men and Elves.

DIGGING DEEPER

The Men of Númenor, or Númenóreans, *were* the Atlanteans, as Tolkien makes clear by referring to the island, after it is destroyed, as Atalantë. Plato invented the myth of Atlantis in his *Timaeus* and *Critias*, and he used it, as Tolkien did, as an object lesson for how human pride and rebellion lead to destruction.

Tolkien developed that theme further by linking his Númenóreans to the Egyptians, both of whom channeled their obsession with mortality into building huge tombs to their dead kings and accumulating vast wealth. Tolkien explained in his letters that the key theme of *The*

Lord of the Rings was death and immortality, and that struggle is captured powerfully in the refusal of the Númenóreans to accept death as the gift of Ilúvatar.

The same dynamic recurs in book four, chapter five of *The Lord of the Rings*, when Faramir explains to Frodo how the Men of Gondor made the same error as their ancestors:

"Death was ever present, because the Númenóreans [of Gondor] still, as they had in their old kingdom [of Númenor], and so lost it, hungered after endless life unchanging. Kings made tombs more splendid than houses of the living, and counted old names in the rolls of their descent dearer than the names of sons. Childless lords sat in aged halls musing on heraldry; in secret chambers withered men compounded strong elixirs, or in high cold towers asked questions of the stars. And the last king of the line of Anárion had no heir."

Rather than channel their yearning for immortality into begetting offspring that will carry on their name, they cease to have children and focus only on unnaturally extending their lives. Gollum and the Nazgûl achieve just such a false immortality, only to find themselves trapped in living deaths that have quantity but no quality, breath but no life.

In the glory days of Númenor, the good kings, when they sensed the end of their life was approaching, passed on their crown to their son and accepted their death as the gift of Ilúvatar, releasing them from the circles of this world. This should not be confused with suicide, which is condemned in Christianity and the legendarium. It is, rather, like Jesus on the cross giving up his spirit willingly and commending it to God (Luke 23:46).

Despite the connections to the pagan Atlanteans and Egyptians, the Númenóreans were monotheists who worshipped Ilúvatar. In the center of the island, on top of Mount Meneltarma ("The Pillar of Heaven"), they marked off a sacred place open to the air on which there was neither temple nor altar. Three times per year, the kings ascended to the summit, where they offered praise, prayer, and thanksgiving to Ilúvatar. To aid the Men of Númenor in their rites, Manwë sent three Eagles from Valinor to guard Meneltarma.

Only when they had been corrupted by Sauron did they erect an altar on Meneltarma and act as devotees of a pagan cult. After the manner of the Gnostics of the early Church, Sauron fooled them into believing the one they called Creator (Ilúvatar) was an evil God.

After Númenor sank beneath the sea, it was said that the summit of Meneltarma, where Ilúvatar had once been worshipped, yet stood above the foam. For this reason, Faramir and his Rangers faced toward that sacred summit in a moment of silence before they ate.

Just as Tolkien gave Númenor a name that links it to Atlantis, so he linked Tol Eressëa to the England of legend by naming a city on the island Avallónë. Avalon is the island where King Arthur is said to remain asleep until the world needs him again. Both Avalon and Atlantis provoked in Tolkien that very elegiac sense of nostalgia, longing, and loss that provides the dominant mood of *The Silmarillion* and *The Lord of the Rings*.

". . . the fear of death grew ever darker upon them, and they delayed it by all means that they could; and they began to build great houses for their dead, while their wise men laboured unceasingly to discover if they might the secret of recalling life, or at the least of the prolonging of Men's days. Yet they achieved only the art of preserving incorrupt the dead flesh of Men, and they filled all the land with silent tombs in which the thought of death was enshrined in the darkness. But those that lived turned the more eagerly to pleasure and revelry, desiring ever more goods and more riches . . ." (*The Silmarillion, Akallabêth*).

". . . and Númenor went down into the sea, with all its children and its wives and its maidens and its ladies proud; and all its gardens and its halls and its towers, its tombs and its riches, and its jewels and its webs and its things painted and carven, and its laughter and its mirth and its music, its wisdom and its lore: they vanished forever. . . . And all the coasts and seaward regions of the western world suffered great change and ruin in that time; for the seas invaded the lands, and shores foundered, and ancient isles were drowned, and new isles were uplifted; and hills crumbled and rivers were turned into strange courses" (*The Silmarillion, Akallabêth*).

EIGHT

Lost and Unfinished Tales

AFTER THE POSITIVE RECEPTION of *The Silmarillion*, Christopher Tolkien devoted the next four decades to gathering and publishing stories, notes, and ideas from his father's manuscripts that broaden and flesh out the full depth and breadth of the legendarium. Various insights from the many volumes published by Christopher have already found their way into the previous six chapters and will do so in the ones that follow.

To give a clearer sense of how these volumes can enrich one's reading of Tolkien's works, I will show here how the two volumes by Christopher that, to my mind, offer the most new material and provide new perspectives on the tales recorded in *The Silmarillion*.

The Book of Lost Tales Part One

The Valar are referred to as gods, and Ilúvatar is presented as a Lord who always and ever lives beyond the world he made. He loves the world but is not of it.

Tolkien had experimented with a different way of telling the stories of *The Silmarillion*. He imagines that Men can still catch a glimpse of Valinor and so be filled with a longing and a yearning for the west. Eriol, driven by such a longing, visits Tol Eressëa where he is told the tales of the First Age over a series of nights, inducing a nostalgic mood of loss.

Eriol longs to be one of the Elves, but he is told that Men and Elves are of a different kind. If Eriol drinks an elvish draught, he will become an Elf, but at a high price. A time will come when he will long to return to the world of Men but will not be able to.

Melkor is a Pandora figure whose fatal curiosity ushers pain and discord into the world.

Melkor uses a divide and conquer method to weaken the collective force of the other Valar. He tries to separate them in accordance with their elements (earth, air, water), but Aulë, suspicious of Melkor's motives, foils his plans by building a great dwelling place to keep the Valar together.

Melkor fools the other Valar by speaking to them sweetly and fairly (as Sauron does on Númenor and Saruman and Wormtongue do in *Lord of the Rings*). He pretends to help the Valar build the Two Lamps to light Middle-earth so that he can secure them on pillars of ice. As a result, when the ice grows warm and melts, a deluge wipes away the Lamps.

The birth of the Two Trees is made possible by the construction of two cauldrons that collect light from air and water. Out of these pits of light, the Trees sprout and grow.

Ilúvatar gives to Men the gift of freedom, allowing them even to add to the song of the Ainur. Ilúvatar lets Men misuse their free will, but he always remains in control.

The Valar bring the three patriarchs of the Elves to meet with them shortly after their birth, though the Elves themselves remember nothing of their birth. To the Elves, all seems a dream. Because the Valar did not take part in the Song of Ilúvatar that brought the Elves to life, they often find it hard to understand them.

It might have been better had the Elves never come to Valinor, though, had they not, they would never have been exposed to the beauty, mystery, and magic of the Valar.

It is only after the Elves are born that the Valar realize that they have desired and longed for them and that the world was somehow empty before they came.

The Elves not only dig gems out of the earth; they make them out of the fair substances around them. Fëanor, for example, gathers light from Valinor to make the Silmarils. They give many of the gems they create to the Valar, who delight in them. Only Melkor is not given any gems, an oversight which furthers his jealousy and hatred of the Elves.

Melkor uses his deceitful tongue to convince the Elves that they are the slaves of the Valar and that Valinor is not Eden but a prison.

Unfinished Tales

Túrin had an elf-like sister who was filled with joy and laughter, but she died young due to the evil breath of Morgoth. Túrin, who was already moody and impulsive, became even more so and swore vengeance against Morgoth.

Young Túrin becomes friends with Sador and asks him many questions about fate and death, Men and Elves. Sador says that it would perhaps have been better had the Edain never met the Elves, for the Elves make the lives of Men seem shorter and more bitter in comparison. At the age of eight, Túrin cries out that he wishes he were an Elf and did not have to die. Sadly, Túrin eventually dies by his own hand.

After he flees the ruins of Nargothrond, Túrin returns to Hithlum, where he is reunited with Sador and leads a rebellion against the Men corrupted by Morgoth. Alas, his noble but rash actions lead only to the death of Sador and the abandonment of Hithlum.

When Húrin is chained to the chair by Morgoth and interrogated, he responds as if he were a martyr of the early Church. Morgoth, he exclaims boldly, is not the creator of Middle-earth but a Valar who chose the path of corruption. Morgoth may kill him, but he does not have the power to pursue Men beyond the circles of the world.

After his mother dies of grief over the death of her husband, Tuor is raised in hiding by Elves. One day, however, he fights with a group of Orcs, is captured, and lives as a slave for three years. Eventually he escapes, and, like Beren and Túrin, lives as an outlaw.

But he is ever drawn by joy and desire to reach Turgon in Gondolin as his father and uncle once had done. In his long search, he makes his way to the Firth of Drengist, the cove on the shore of Beleriand where Fëanor arrived with his Teleri ships. He thus becomes the first Man to gaze on the great western sea. He then follows a flock of gulls to Nevrast where he is met by Ulmo who commissions him to seek out Gondolin. On his way there, he passes Túrin on his way from Nargothrond to Hithlum.

Meneldur, the fifth king of Númenor, possesses a deep love for astronomy, but his son Aldarion is a lover of the sea. Aldarion builds many ships and ports and havens and often sails with his grandfather Elendil to the western coast of Middle-earth. There he befriends Gil-Galad and Círdan and often advises and aids them against the dangers of Sauron's shadow rising in the east.

Alas, though he is accounted an Elf-friend, he is resented by his father and by his wife Erendis. As great as his yearning is for the sea and his indomitable wanderlust, so is Erendis's passion to care for the trees and the sheep of Númenor. During their courtship, Erendis waits for long periods of time as Aldarion sails off again and again to Middle-earth. In the end, she convinces Aldarion to marry her.

Though her mother warns her to support her husband rather than seek to trim his fire, she increasingly resents Aldarion's voyages. As the years pass, she grows colder and more bitter, while Aldarion waxes proud and willful, refusing to be tied down by his wife. After Aldarion's promise of a two-year journey expands into five, Erendis withdraws from the court and retires to the countryside with their daughter Ancalimë. There she raises her in a quiet house of women, cut off from the loud, boisterous voices of men.

When Aldarion returns from Middle-earth, where he had been helping Gil-Galad, she gives him a cold homecoming and the two separate. Meneldur remains angry with his son, until he receives a letter from Gil-Galad praising Aldarion. Then Meneldur, who could not himself solve the dilemma of whether to stay isolated on Númenor or send warriors to Middle-earth, steps back and gives the crown to Aldarion.

Thus father and son are reconciled, but not husband and wife. The sorrow in this tale of polarized masculinity and femininity is terribly sad, but it shows Tolkien's insight into human nature and the differences between men and women that often plague marriage. He may, in fact, have loosely based the tale on his own marriage to Edith, which was not always happy due to their very different interests and approaches to life. In a letter he wrote to his son Michael on March 6–8, 1941, he offers practical advice about the sexes that reflects the insights of his melancholy tale of Aldarion and Erendis.

"A man has a life-work, a career, (and male friends), all of which could (and do where he has any guts) survive the shipwreck of 'love.' A young woman, even one 'economically independent' . . . begins to think of the 'bottom drawer' and dream of a home, almost at once. . . . Anyway women are in general much less romantic and more practical. Don't be misled by the fact that they are more 'sentimental' in words—freer with 'darling,' and all that. They do not want a guiding star. They may idealize a plain young man into a hero; but they don't really need any such glamour either to fall in love or to remain in it. If they have any delusion it is that they can 'reform' men."

NINE

The Third Age of Middle-earth

○

Sauron fortifies **Dol Guldur** in **Greenwood**, which becomes **Mirkwood**.

Wizards **Saruman** the White, **Gandalf** the Grey, **Radagast** the Brown are sent.

Minas Ithil falls and becomes **Minas Morgul**, Tower of Black Magic;

Minas Anor remains and becomes **Minas Tirith**, Tower of the Guard.

White Council forms: Saruman (leader), Gandalf, **Elrond**, **Galadriel**.

Eärnur, last King of Gondor, is killed by the **Witch King of Angmar**.

Sméagol kills **Déagol** to possess Ring, then lives beneath Misty Mountains.

Celebrían, wife of Elrond, is injured and leaves Middle-earth.

Cirion, Steward of Gondor, is aided by **Eorl the Young** and grants him Rohan.

Keys of **Orthanc** are given to **Saruman**.

White Council drives Sauron out of Dol Guldur, but Saruman betrays Council.

○

(This overview of the Third Age leading up to the time of the War of the Ring is based on the final chapter of *The Silmarillion* and the appendices to *The Lord of the Rings*.)

Although Sauron is defeated at the end of the Second Age, because the Ring was not destroyed, his spirit endures and slowly regains its form and power. By the year 1000 of the Third Age, he is strong enough to extend his reach from Mordor to the forest of Greenwood, which lies on the east side of the great River Anduin, across from Rivendell to the north and Lothlórien, the forest home of Galadriel and Celeborn, to the south. He establishes his stronghold at Dol Guldur in the southwest corner of Greenwood, and a shadow falls over the forest that causes the Men of the region to refer to it as Mirkwood.

Gandalf   Saruman   Radagast

About this time, the Valar, fearing that Sauron will once again envelop Middle-earth in darkness, send the Istari, or Wizards, to help protect Middle-earth from Sauron. They are spiritual beings incarnated in the forms of old but vigorous bearded Men. Though possessed of special powers, the Valar, who feel guilt for the mistakes they made in seeking to control the Elves, forbid them from seeking or holding power in Middle-earth.

Their leader, Saruman the White, grows close in the counsels of Men, while Gandalf the Grey consults most often with the Elves. Radagast the Brown prefers the company of animals, while the names and deeds of the remaining two Blue Wizards are lost.

Over the next thousand years, the Nazgûl reappear, and the northern

Kingdom of Arnor is lost. Osgiliath falls into ruins and Minas Ithil is abandoned. At Minas Anor, the heirs of Anárion rule as kings, while the heirs of Isildur become wandering Rangers in the north.

In the year 2002, the Nazgûl seize Minas Ithil, changing its name to Minas Morgul, the Tower of Black Magic. In response, Minas Anor becomes Minis Tirith, the Tower of the Guard, and keeps its long watch on Mordor. Shortly thereafter, Eärnur, the last king of Gondor, rides east to face the head of the Nazgûl, the Witch King of Angmar, although he knows the prophecy that no man can defeat him. He is never heard from again.

For the next thousand years, Gondor is ruled by a succession of Stewards, whose commission it is to guard and rule Gondor until the return of the true king. Since the line of Anárion is now gone, that heir can only come from the line of Isildur.

A Watchful Peace follows that lasts for nearly five centuries, until it is broken by Sauron's return to Dol Goldur in 1460. To guard Middle-earth from Sauron, the White Council is formed; it is led by Saruman and includes Gandalf, Galadriel, and Elrond.

About this time, a Hobbit-like creature named Déagol goes fishing in the Anduin, near the Gladden Fields where Isildur had been killed by Orcs. Dragged under the water by a great fish that pulls on his hook, Déagol reaches out his hand and grasps the Ring. But his friend Sméagol, whose birthday it is, demands the Ring as his present. When Déagol refuses, Sméagol strangles his friend and steals the Ring.

Though the Ring makes him invisible and extends his life indefinitely, it cuts him off from his family and friends and transforms him into a loathsome creature that fears and hates the light and all things good and fair. Because he mutters and gurgles in his throat, he comes to be known as Gollum.

The Ring drives him underground away from the light in search of forbidden secrets. In the end, he comes to live deep under the Misty Mountains where he feeds on raw fish and is forgotten by the world.

MMMM

About this time as well, two other events of note occur. Celebrían, who bore to Elrond Arwen and sons Elladan and Elrohir, is traveling to Lothlórien to visit her parents when she receives a poisonous wound from a party of Orcs. The wound does not kill her, but she grows dark and morose and abandons Elrond, departing over the sea to Valinor.

Cirion, twelfth and noblest of the Stewards of Gondor, perceives the growing strength of the enemy and calls for aid from the Rohirrim, the great horse riders of Rohan, who also descended from the Númenóreans and are thus distant kinsmen of the Men of Gondor. Their brave leader, Eorl the Young, answers the call and saves Cirion and his men at the Battle of the Field of Celebrant, which lies north of Gondor by the Anduin.

As a reward, Cirion gives Eorl and his people the region of Rohan. It stretches north from the White Mountains to the Forest of Fangorn and west from the Anduin to the Gap of Rohan, which stands between the foot of the Misty Mountains, where lies Isengard, and the start of the White Mountains that run east to the Anduin. At its eastern end, where it touches the Anduin, the Men of Gondor build the mighty White Tower of Minas Tirith.

In return for the land, Eorl swears an oath that if ever Gondor is in need, Rohan will come. A succession of beacons is built by which Gondor can signal Rohan in times of danger. Though Gondor keeps for herself the keys of Orthanc, she later entrusts them to Saruman so that she can focus her watchfulness on threats from Mordor in the east.

In 2941, the year of Bilbo's journey, the White Council drives Sauron out of Dol Goldur, but Saruman betrays the Council and begins to search for the Ring by the Anduin.

TEN

The Hobbit

Bilbo Baggins of the Shire joins **Gandalf** and
Thirteen Dwarves led by **Thorin Oakenshield.**
He meets **Elrond** in Rivendell and **Gollum** in the Misty
   Mountains;
He faces **Wolves, Goblins** (that is, **Orcs**), and **Spiders;**
He stays with **Beorn**, a shape shifter who is a Man and a
   Bear;
He rescues the Dwarves from **Thranduil** of the woodland
   Elves.
Gandalf and the White Council chase the **Necromancer**
   (**Sauron**) out of Dol Guldur.
Bilbo meets with **Smaug** the dragon in Erebor and learns
   his weak spot,
So that **Bard** of Lake-town can kill him with an arrow.
Bilbo steals the **Arkenstone** but then gives it up to bring
   reconciliation.
The Battle of Five Armies includes Men, Elves, Dwarves,
   Goblins, and Wolves.

THE TALE

Bilbo Baggins was a Hobbit who lived in the Shire in the northwest
region of Middle-earth. Like all Hobbits, he lived a simple, petty-bour-
geois life, eating seven meals a day and enjoying his creature comforts.
That is, until Gandalf arrived and invited him to go on an adventure.
Before he knew it, his neat little Hobbit hole at Bag-End was invaded

by thirteen Dwarves led by Thorin Oakenshield, grandson of the King under the Mountain.

The king had been forced to flee from his stronghold in Erebor, the Lonely Mountain, by the Dragon Smaug, and Thorin was determined to return and reclaim his kingdom and his treasure. He had with him a map and key that would allow him to enter a secret passage on the side of Erebor and so surprise Smaug. Bilbo was just the burglar for the job!

Bilbo had no love for adventures, but, as he heard the Dwarves sing of mountains and gold, something courageous woke up inside of him, and he agreed. He proved a good companion, saving the company, with Gandalf's help, from three Trolls and uncovering a trove of weapons, from which he acquired the blade that he would later name Sting.

The company traveled east from the Shire until they came to Rivendell, where they were shown hospitality by Elrond, who also taught them how to read the map. They planned to cross the Misty Mountains, since Erebor lay east of the northeast corner of Mirkwood, but storm and stone-giants prevented them from crossing. Thus were they forced to travel south and cross under the mountains by way of the Goblin-infested Mines of Moria.

It was here that something unusual happened to Bilbo that would change his life forever. He fell through a crack in the earth and found himself in the deep cave where Gollum had been living for five hundred years. By chance, the Ring had fallen from Gollum's finger, and, also by chance, Bilbo had found it and put it in his pocket. When Gollum became aware of the intruder, he challenged him to a riddle contest, planning to eat him if he lost. But Bilbo won, and he demanded Gollum fulfill his promise and show him the way out.

Instead, Gollum ran to find his Ring so that he could become invisible and strangle Bilbo. When he found it was gone, he screamed out in pain. Again by chance, Bilbo put on the Ring and discovered he was invisible. Angered by Gollum's treachery, he almost killed him, but then stopped himself out of pity for the miserable creature.

Reunited with the company, Bilbo was rescued by Eagles from a pack of Wolves and stayed with Beorn, a Man-Bear shape shifter. While crossing Mirkwood, Bilbo and company were attacked by spiders and imprisoned by woodland Elves led by Thranduil. But Bilbo used his Ring of invisibility to rescue them from Thranduil's dungeon and float them down the river on barrels to Lake-town, a city of Men not far from Erebor.

Gandalf was not with the company at this point because he had left to join the White Council and drive the Necromancer (Sauron) out of Dol Guldur in southwest Mirkwood.

The Men of Lake-town hailed Thorin as King under the Mountain, little knowing that he would bring destruction to their town in the form of Smaug, who was roused to anger when Bilbo entered through the secret passage and stole a cup from his treasure trove. Luckily, Bilbo, rendered invisible by his Ring, had met and spoken with Smaug and discovered a weak spot in his scales. The knowledge of the weak spot was carried by a thrush from Bilbo to Bard, who used the information to kill Smaug with an arrow.

Meanwhile, Thorin ransacked Smaug's cave and took all of its jewels, though Bilbo secretly took the Arkenstone, the Heart of the Mountain, the greatest treasure of the kings of Erebor.

When Thorin allowed his possessive greed for Smaug's treasure to set him at enmity with Thranduil and the Men of Lake-town, Bilbo bravely and selflessly offered up the Arkenstone as a bargaining tool to bring reconciliation. But Thorin would not share his treasure and demanded as well the Arkenstone as his sole possession.

As a result, war broke out between Men, Elves, and Dwarves, though they were forced to unite when Goblins and Wolves attacked them to secure Smaug's treasure. The Goblins and Wolves might have won the Battle of the Five Armies had not a squadron of Eagles arrived in the nick of time. In the battle, Thorin was mortally wounded; however, before he died, he asked Bilbo's pardon and commended him for his courage and wisdom.

Bilbo returned to the Shire a rich man, only to find that his relatives were in the process of auctioning off Bag-End and his possessions! Still, all ended well, though Gandalf reminded Bilbo that his adventures were not due to luck but to a greater providence.

DIGGING DEEPER

Unlike *The Silmarillion* and *The Lord of the Rings*, *The Hobbit* is a children's story that is far lighter in tone and mood. It bears the subtitle "There and Back Again," for Bilbo is able to return unscathed from his adventures and take up his old life again. He changes and matures over the course of his quest-journey, and he encounters some troubles when he returns, but the world as he knows it is not turned upside down. Such is not the case for Frodo, who is deeply wounded and experiences massive social and political upheaval.

Still, in both *The Hobbit* and *The Lord of the Rings*, Tolkien focuses on an unlikely hero who demonstrates strength in weakness and wisdom in humility. Bilbo and Frodo are like the younger sons in Genesis or David or Israel itself: the smallest of the small chosen to fulfill a mighty destiny. The petit-bourgeois Bilbo and Frodo, with their love of simple pleasures and risk-aversive approach to life, seem lacking in the qualities necessary for a hero; yet, they step out of their comfort zone and show great courage. This is especially true of Bilbo, who, we might say, is a provincial grocer from a nation of shopkeepers.

The Hobbit functions as a warm-up for *The Lord of the Rings* in a number of ways.

First, Bilbo follows the same basic geographical route that Frodo will take: a westward march from the Shire to Rivendell punctuated by danger (the Trolls for Bilbo; the Nazgûl for Frodo); an aborted attempt to cross over the Misty Mountains that forces a dangerous underground journey through the Mines of Moria; a trek through a forest (Mirkwood for Bilbo; Lothlórien for Frodo) followed by a journey on water (Bilbo on the barrels; Frodo down the Anduin); a slog through a wasted area (the Desolation of Smaug; Mordor); a descent into a cave (Smaug's lair; the Cracks of Doom); and a return trip to the Shire.

Second, the hero makes his way through a landscape marked by great age and multiple layers of history. Though the layering is less pronounced in *The Hobbit*, references are made to the First and Second Ages of Middle-earth and to the doings of Elves, Dwarfs, Númenóreans, and Wizards. This is a "lived-in" world, and the narrator must restrain himself from going off on endless tangents. Only in *The Lord of the Rings* will we realize the enormous importance of the Ring and of Gandalf's struggles with the Necromancer.

Third, in Thorin's lust for the Arkenstone, and the battle that ensues because of his greed, we catch a glimpse of the corrupting power of the Ring. Middle-earth is a place where virtue and vice are in constant struggle, and the decisions of characters have far-ranging consequences. Good and evil are embodied in these choices as well as in rational creatures who seek to live in harmony with nature and others (Men, Elves, Dwarves, Hobbits, and Eagles) or in conflict with both (Goblins/Orcs, Wolves, and Spiders).

Fourth, Thorin foreshadows both Aragorn and Boromir. He is like Aragorn in that he is a messianic king returning to regain his lost kingdom and set things to rights. When he first comes to Lake-town (chapter ten), he is greeted with this song: "The streams shall run in gladness, / The lakes shall shine and burn, / All sorrow fail and sadness, / At the Mountain-king's return!" He is like Boromir in that, though his lust for the Arkenstone leads to his death, he sees the error of his ways and dies forgiven and reconciled.

Fifth, both Bilbo and Frodo are defined by the pity they show to Gollum and by their ability to move out of themselves to help others. They possess the biblical virtue of meekness, which does not mean weakness but a kind of firm patience and strong humility that rises above injury and resentment to reach out to others with gentleness. Bilbo also shows this in his willingness to give up the priceless Arkenstone and to forgive and rescue the Dwarves despite their often unkind treatment of him.

Sixth, though God does not appear in either novel, he is there in the form of a guiding providence. What seems like luck always turns out to be part of a deeper design. Good and bad magic exist in both novels, and they are linked, if sometimes obscurely, to greater powers of goodness (Valar and Wizards) and of evil (Sauron and Morgoth).

I've left 'divine intervention' out of the story. I show that evil is fought by the combined efforts of free peoples. But there is a *guiding providence*.

Seventh, though both novels introduce us to all manner of strange creatures and magical places, they are ever seen through the eyes of humble Hobbits with whom we can relate. The fact that this perspective is missing in *The Silmarillion* has made it less accessible.

"As they sang the hobbit felt the love of beautiful things made by hands and by cunning and by magic moving through him, a fierce and jealous love, the desire of the hearts of the Dwarves. Then something Tookish woke up inside him, and he wished to go and see the great mountains, and hear the pine-trees and the waterfalls, and explore the caves, and wear a sword instead of a walking-stick" (*The Hobbit*, chapter one).

"He must stab the foul thing, put its eyes out, kill it. It meant to kill him. No, not a fair fight. He was invisible now. Gollum had no sword. Gollum had not actually threatened to kill him, or tried to yet. And he was miserable, alone, lost. A sudden understanding, a pity mixed with horror, welled up in Bilbo's heart: a glimpse of endless unmarked days without light or hope of betterment, hard stone, cold fish, sneaking and whispering. All these thoughts passed in a flash of a second. He trembled. And then quite suddenly in another flash, as if lifted by a new strength and resolve, he leaped" (*The Hobbit*, chapter five).

[Thorin's dying words to Bilbo] "There is more in you of good than you know, child of the kindly West. Some courage and some wisdom, blended in measure. If more of us valued food and cheer and song above hoarded gold, it would be a merrier world. But sad or merry, I must leave it now. Farewell" (*The Hobbit*, chapter eighteen).

[Gandalf's final words to Bilbo] "Surely you don't disbelieve the prophecies, because you had a hand in bringing them about yourself? You don't really suppose, do you, that all your adventures and escapes were managed by mere luck, just for your sole benefit? You are a very fine person, Mr. Baggins, and I am very fond of you; but you are only quite a little fellow in a wide world after all!" "Thank goodness!" said Bilbo laughing . . ." (*The Hobbit*, chapter nineteen).

ELEVEN

The Lord of the Rings I:
From the Shire to Rivendell

✪

Bilbo Baggins celebrates his 111th birthday in the Shire,
Then leaves for Rivendell, entrusting the Ring to **Frodo
 Baggins.**
Gandalf discovers it is the One Ring and that **Sauron,**
Informed by **Gollum,** has sent the **Nazgûl** to the Shire to find
 the Ring.
Frodo and Samwise (**Sam**) Gamgee flee to the Prancing
 Pony in Bree
With Meriadoc (**Merry**) Brandybuck and Peregrin (**Pippin**)
 Took.
On the way, they visit the Old Forest and meet **Tom
 Bombadil** and **Goldberry;**
They are almost killed by a **Barrow-wight** at the
 Barrow-downs.
In Bree, they meet a Ranger named **Strider** who leads them
 to Rivendell.
On Weathertop, Frodo is stabbed by the **Witch King** of the
 Nazgûl,
But he is taken safely to Rivendell by the Elf **Glorfindel.**

✪

THE TALE

Sixty-one years after the events of *The Hobbit,* Bilbo celebrated his 111th birthday in the Shire. Because of the influence of the Ring, he looked scarcely older than he had at fifty. Though he had been careful not to use the Ring, he used its power of invisibility one last time at the party to slip out of the Shire and head for Rivendell. He came close to taking the Ring with him, but Gandalf convinced him to leave it behind for Frodo Baggins.

At the time Frodo was thirty-three years old and was not ready to leave the Shire as his uncle had. For the next seventeen years, Gandalf, troubled by the Ring's hold on Bilbo, searched through the ancient records, only to discover that Frodo's Ring was the One Ring of Sauron

Leave it for Frodo, there's a good hobbit.

that had passed down from Isildur to Gollum to Bilbo to Frodo.

He also learned that Gollum had been captured by Sauron—who had returned to Mordor after the White Council had driven him out of Dol Guldur—and tortured until he revealed the name of Bilbo Baggins and the Shire. Sauron had then dispatched the Nazgûl to seek out the Ring in the Shire. As a result, Frodo, now fifty, was forced to flee in the company of his faithful gardener Samwise (Sam) Gamgee. Along the way, they were joined by two other Hobbits: Meriadoc (Merry) Brandybuck and Peregrin (Pippin) Took.

As they made their way to the Prancing Pony, where Gandalf had promised to meet them, they were almost captured by a Ring-wraith in the form of a Black Rider, helped by Farmer Maggot, whose dogs had terrified the young Frodo, and nearly killed by Old Man Willow in the Old Forest. They were rescued by the jolly but mysterious Tom Bombadil, and his wife Goldberry, who was unaffected by the Ring's power. He rescued them again when they were almost killed by a ghostly Barrow-wight that haunted the Barrow-downs.

When the Hobbits reached Bree, Gandalf was not there. Instead, they were taken under the wing of a Ranger named Strider, who is actually the heir of Isildur and thus the long-awaited king of Gondor and Arnor. Strider guided them to Rivendell. On the summit of Weathertop, they were attacked by Black Riders. Frodo put on the Ring, allowing him to see the Black Riders as the spectral, undead zombies they are. Doing so, however, made him vulnerable, and he was stabbed by the Witch King with a poisonous blade.

With the Nazgûl in pursuit, Frodo was carried to Rivendell by an Elf named Glorfindel. After he crossed the ford to the edge of Rivendell, Elrond used his magic to catch the Black Riders in a flood that killed their steeds and incapacitated them for many months.

DIGGING DEEPER

Hobbits on the Road

Throughout the epic, the Road, which Tolkien always capitalizes, plays a prominent role. It beckons the characters, promising them both adventure and danger.

> [Bilbo] "used often to say there was only one Road; that it was like a great river: its springs were at every doorstep, and every path was its tributary. 'It's a dangerous business, Frodo, going out your door,' he used to say. 'You step into the Road, and if you don't keep your feet,

there is no knowing where you might be swept off to'" (book one, chapter three).[3]

In Tolkien's legendarium, we are all finally pilgrims, resident aliens in the world, seeking after our true home. In that sense, *The Lord of the Rings* stands in the same tradition as *The Odyssey*, *The Aeneid*, *The Divine Comedy*, *Don Quixote*, *Pilgrim's Progress*, and *Huckleberry Finn*, not to mention Genesis, Exodus, and Acts.

As a WWI veteran, Tolkien knew how to march, and his characters do a lot of marching through the landscapes of Middle-earth. In that sense, the Road is a teacher and drill sergeant that toughens up the pilgrims and keeps them focused on their task. What sets *The Lord of the Rings* apart from the other works, including *The Hobbit*, is that whereas

---

3 Henceforth, I shall cite passages from *The Lord of the Rings* by the book number in Roman numerals and the chapter in Arabic numerals. Thus, book one, chapter one will be written as I.3.

most pilgrims go on a quest to find a prize, Frodo goes on a quest to destroy a prize.

It is ironic that provincial, stay-at-home Hobbits who are suspicious of people in the next village should be the ones to lead this "anti-quest," but that is because their simple, merry exteriors conceal a remarkable toughness and capacity to endure. They are like the rural, slightly xenophobic, often stubborn Englishmen who fought with Tolkien in WWI and then rose up again in WWII to stand alone in Europe against the threat of totalitarianism.

Pity and Providence

As Gandalf explains to Frodo the history of the Ring, two themes from *The Hobbit* appear that take on greater prominence in *The Lord of the Rings*. First, when Frodo says it was a pity Bilbo did not kill Gollum when he had the chance, Gandalf responds that it *was* pity that prevented Bilbo from killing him and that he was not corrupted by the Ring the way Gollum was because he began his possession of the Ring by showing pity to its previous owner. Frodo counters that Gollum deserves death, to which Gandalf replies:

> "Deserves it! I daresay he does. Many that live deserve death. And
> some that die deserve life. Can you give it to them? Then do not
> be too eager to deal out death in judgement. For even the very wise
> cannot see all ends. I have not much hope that Gollum can be cured
> before he dies, but there is a chance of it. And he is bound up with
> the fate of the Ring. My heart tells me he has some part to play yet,
> for good or ill, before the end; and when that comes, the pity of Bilbo
> may rule the fate of many—yours not least" (I.2).

For Tolkien, the extension of pity is motivated by the hope that its object will reform, as Gandalf clings to the hope that Saruman, or at least Wormtongue, will reform. In the case of Gollum, Gandalf senses that Gollum is so tied up with the fate of the Ring that the decision to kill him would betray a prideful attempt to discern the ways of providence.

In fact, when Frodo exclaims that he wishes these things had not happened in his own time, Gandalf responds gently:

> "So do I . . . and so do all who live to see such times. But that is not for them to decide. All we have to decide is what to do with the time that is given us" (I.2).

We are not the masters of our own fate, but we *do* possess free will and must use it to respond properly to the challenges and duties laid before us. Just so, Esther did not choose to be lifted up to the role of queen of Persia at the very time Xerxes, pushed by an evil counselor, was planning to wipe out her fellow Jews. She would have preferred to remain safe and silent, but her uncle Mordecai told her that it was at this very time and for this very reason, to save her people, that she was given her position of influence (Esther 4).

The Ring

In the broadest sense, the Ring represents Original Sin (innate human depravity). That is why it plays on the pride and lust for power of all the characters who come near it. In a more narrow sense, it highlights numerous aspects of sin. First, like the Tree of the Knowledge of Good and of Evil in the Garden of Eden, it offers the lure of forbidden wisdom. In the end, that secret wisdom proves empty and hollow, but the possessor does not realize that until he has sold his soul to acquire it.

Second, it offers to protect and exalt those who put their trust in it. But it is a weapon that must not be used, for it is a weapon that consumes its wielder. It does give power, but that power does the wielder no good, for, in grasping the Ring, he loses his selfhood.

Third, it often corrupts its wearers by playing on their virtues. Saruman desires to use the Ring to bring order, but, had he gained it, he would have become as tyrannical as Sauron. Galadriel would have used it to keep Middle-earth in a perpetual state of beauty with herself as the queen, but she would have demanded that all worship her and her vision. Gandalf would have used it for pity and a desire to do good and so become the worst tyrant of all—one who crushes freedom while convincing himself his motives are pure.

Defending the Slow Pace

Even a Tolkien fan must admit book one moves at a snail's pace. Part of the reason for that slowness is that Tolkien didn't really know where his book was heading when he started writing it. When the first Black Rider showed up, it took Tolkien the author by surprise.

But the slow development accomplishes something else. Readers who will soon witness the suffering, death, and despair caused by the War of the Ring must know *why* the battle is being fought. The more time we have to fall in love with the Hobbits and the Shire, the more we understand what exactly is at stake and why it is worth the sacrifice of so many.

As for our four Hobbit heroes, before they can participate in so great an adventure, they must cross the border from innocence to experience. The mysterious Black Rider in his dark cloak, the phobia over Farmer Maggot's dogs, the thick wood that conceals dangers, the threatening trees, the ghost that haunts the graveyard: these are the primal fears of childhood we all must face and overcome if we are to move into a healthy adulthood.

Goldberry

Tom Bombadil

As for the tangential adventure with Tom Bombadil, it does serve some purposes in terms of the narrative. Tom and Goldberry prepare us to meet Treebeard and Galadriel while reminding us that Middle-earth is very old and filled with inexhaustible wonders. Indeed, Bombadil, who is neither tempted nor affected by the Ring (it does not render him invisible when he puts it on!), reminds us that not all of Middle-earth is part of the War of the Ring. To Bombadil, who seems to live in a state of grace, the Ring is only a toy.

Bree and the Rangers

Bree is presented as an archetypal border town, the kind one sees in Westerns. It stands on the threshold of civilization and the wilderness, allowing commerce between all types and races. The Inn of the Prancing Pony is a "Wild West" saloon where it is not easy to distinguish friend from foe. Like the Hobbits themselves, Strider is someone whose inner courage and integrity are not reflected by his rough exterior: gold does not always glitter.

In terms of the legendarium, the Rangers are the last remnants of the Númenóreans of the north. Archetypally speaking, they are the lonely, isolated cowboys or knights or samurai or marines who protect civilization while being ignored or despised by the very people they protect. The Hobbits can only live their idyllic, sheltered life because of the perpetual vigilance of the Rangers, who guard them from unseen foes that would chill their blood. They may wander, but they are not lost; they know their duty and fulfill it.

TWELVE

The Lord of the Rings II:
The Fellowship of the Ring

At the Council of **Elrond** in Rivendell we learn that
Gandalf had been imprisoned by **Saruman**, who is now in
league with **Sauron.**
Boromir, son of **Denethor**, Steward of Gondor has come
seeking Isildur's Bane.
Frodo volunteers to take the Ring to Mordor to destroy it;
He is accompanied by Sam, **Merry, Pippin**, Gandalf,
Aragorn, and Boromir.
To fill out the Fellowship, they are joined by the Dwarf **Gimli**
and Elf **Legolas.**
Unable to go over the Misty Mountains, they go through the
Mines of Moria;
Gandalf defeats a **Balrog** but is dragged down with it into
the abyss.
The Fellowship stays with **Galadriel** and **Celeborn** in
Lothlórien.
They boat down the Anduin, see the Argonath, and stop on
the western shore.
Boromir tries to steal the Ring, and Frodo and Sam head to
Mordor alone.

THE TALE

Safe in Rivendell, Frodo was reunited with Bilbo and with Gandalf,
who explained why he had not met him at Bree. Gandalf had gone to
Isengard to seek advice from Saruman, but Saruman had already been

corrupted by Sauron by means of the Isengard palantír that Saruman had discovered. When Gandalf had refused Saruman's offer to join him, find the Ring, and use it to rule Middle-earth, Saruman had imprisoned him on the top of Orthanc. But Gandalf had been rescued by Gwaihir, Lord of the Eagles.

At a council called by Elrond, Frodo met Boromir, son of Denethor, Steward of Gondor. He had journeyed there in response to a riddling prophecy that said he must seek out, in Rivendell, the sword that was broken, where he would see Isildur's Bane held by a Halfling. The Halfling turns out to be Frodo; Isildur's Bane, the Ring that had betrayed Isildur to his death; the broken sword, Narsil, the shards of which Isildur had used to cut the Ring from Sauron's finger and which had been kept at Rivendell for 3,000 years.

Curses!

The council decided that someone must take the Ring to Mordor and do what Isildur had failed to do: throw it into the Cracks of Doom. Only thus could it be unmade and Sauron destroyed. Frodo volunteered, and Elrond assigned him eight companions who would represent all the free peoples of Middle-earth, nine Walkers to defeat the nine Nazgûl.

The Fellowship of the Ring consisted of the four Hobbits, Gandalf, Aragorn, Boromir, Gimli (the son of Glóin, one of the thirteen Dwarves from *The Hobbit*), and Legolas (son of Thranduil, the elf who had imprisoned the thirteen Dwarves). The shards of Narsil were re-forged into Andúril, the Flame of the West, and given to Aragorn, heir of Isildur.

The Fellowship, unable to cross the Misty Mountains, was forced to travel underground through the Mines of Moria. There they were attacked by Orcs and a Balrog that had been driven out by Dwarves who had dug too deeply for mithril ("true silver"). Wielding the power of the Secret Fire of Ilúvatar, Gandalf stopped the Balrog and enabled the Fellowship to escape but was pulled down with the Balrog into the bottomless depths.

The Fellowship escaped to Lothlórien, where they were given shelter by Galadriel and Celeborn. Though Dwarves and Elves had been enemies since the end of the First Age, a growing friendship began here between Gimli and Legolas. While there, Sam and Frodo gazed into Galadriel's Mirror, and Frodo offered the Ring to Galadriel, who refused it.

Galadriel provided the Fellowship with boats to sail down the Anduin, cloaks to render them invisible, and lembas (waybread) to sustain them on their journey. To Frodo, she gave a Phial containing the light of Eärendil's star, which she had collected in her Mirror. To

Sam, she gave a box containing earth from Lothlórien. To Gimli she gave three strands of her golden hair. To Aragorn, she gave a sheath for Andúril, a precious gem, and the messianic title of Elessar, the Elfstone.

As they journeyed down the Anduin, they saw the Argonath, giant statues of Isildur and Anárion; in their shadow, the strength of their heir, Aragorn, was revealed.

They stopped on the west bank of the Anduin to decide whether to head for Mordor or travel to Gondor. As they deliberated, Frodo wandered off, and Boromir, tempted by the Ring, attempted to steal it from Frodo. This forced Frodo to put on the Ring to turn invisible and escape, an action that attracted the attention of the Eye of Sauron.

Without the Ring, Sauron could not assume bodily form. Instead, he guided his armies in the form of a single Eye suspended atop his fortress of Barad-dûr, the Dark Tower, which stood in Mordor, not far from Orodruin, Mount Doom, where the Ring had been forged and where alone it

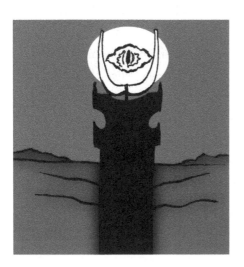

could be destroyed. The Eye called to Frodo to come to him, but, with the help of another voice, Frodo resisted and took off the Ring.

But Frodo knew now that he was a danger to the Fellowship and had to leave. He set off in a boat to travel to Mordor alone, but Sam insisted on accompanying him to the end.

DIGGING DEEPER
Two Kinds of Magic

In the conflict between Gandalf and Saruman, we glimpse two different kinds of magic: one that seeks to work with nature; the other to dominate it. When Gandalf arrives at Isengard, he greets his fellow wizard as Saruman the White, but he says he is now Saruman of Many Colors. When Gandalf says he preferred white, Saruman responds:

> "White!" [Saruman] sneered. "It serves as a beginning. White cloth may be dyed. The white page can be overwritten; and the white light can be broken."
>
> "In which case it is no longer white," said [Gandalf]. "And he that breaks a thing to find out what it is has left the path of wisdom" (II.2).

While Gandalf seeks synthesis, to draw things together into wholeness and integrity, Saruman seeks analysis, breaking things up to uncover, and exploit, their secrets. He seeks to violate and manipulate, not protect and appreciate.

In this distinction between the two wizards, we catch a glimpse of the wider distinction between the sympathetic magic of the Elves and the instrumental magic of Sauron. The Ring is a kind of man-made "machine" that controls rather than enriches rational beings. By such dark magic, Morgoth and Sauron bred Orcs out of Elves; by the same magic, Saruman breeds stronger and more deadly Orcs that can travel in the daylight. Magic here is used as an instrument, a force to conform nature and Man to the will of another.

In sharp contrast, the Elves practice a magic that works with nature. The cloaks they give the Fellowship do not render their wearers invisible by altering or overriding the laws of nature. Rather, they are so imbued with the lore of wood, stone, and water that the wearer who stands or sits by one of these natural elements blends in with it and cannot be seen.

This same kind of deep, elemental magic resides in the lembas that Galadriel gives to the Fellowship, only the second time the elvish waybread was shared with Men. Tolkien associated lembas with the host in the Catholic mass, as he associated Galadriel with the Virgin Mary who ushered the body of Christ (*corpus Christi*) into the world. Its power increases, she tells them, when they rely solely on it for food.

Galadriel's Mirror, a basin which she fills with water, allows those who stare into it to see things from the past, present, and future. When Sam looks, he sees the Shire being laid waste, a prophecy that will come true. Frodo sees the White Tower of Gondor and the White Tree, but then sees, for the first time, the Eye of Sauron. Galadriel explains that seeing is good, but it is also perilous; the Mirror can be a dangerous guide to action.

Just so, the palantíri were created good and had been used properly by the Númenóreans to defend Middle-earth. Sauron and Saruman twisted them into weapons for the purpose of domination. In *The Lord of the Rings*, the lust to know the future is always negative and harmful, for it destroys hope and seeks to control that which cannot be controlled. Tolkien agrees with the Bible, which condemns fortunetelling (Deuteronomy 18:10-14), and Dante, who assigns it a terrible punishment (*Inferno*, canto twenty).

A final clash between sympathetic and instrumental magic takes place between Gandalf and the Balrog. Gandalf calls himself a servant of the Secret Fire, the creative power, ultimately the Holy Spirit, by which Ilúvatar fashioned Arda. Morgoth was never able to steal (Prometheus-like) that Secret Fire, though he lusted after it. Instead, he used the dark fire of his destructive malice to create corrupted creatures like the Orcs and Balrogs. The acquisitive lust of the Dwarves impelled them to dig too deep and wake the Balrog.

Elf and Dwarf

One of the most beautiful aspects of *The Lord of the Rings* is the unique friendship that grows between Gimli and Legolas. It begins with Gimli being won over by the courteousness of Galadriel.

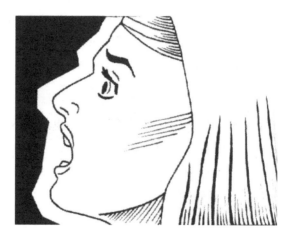

When he enters Lothlórien, the suspicious Elves blindfold Gimli lest he know the secret path into the forest. Celeborn then puts the blame for Gandalf's death on the Dwarves, because they had woken the Balrog of Moria.

Galadriel, however, dispels the bad blood between Elves and Dwarves by speaking gently to Gimli and listing the place-names of Moria in the ancient tongue of the Dwarves. When he hears Galadriel honor the words of his language, Gimli's heart melts, and he finds a friend where he expected an enemy. Later, when Galadriel insists that he ask her for a gift, he asks for a single strand of her hair that he might encase it in crystal as a pledge between Elf and Dwarf. Galadriel, who would not give Fëanor a strand of her hair, gives Gimli three and prays that he will possess much gold but not be possessed by it.

Gimli and Legolas bond over the beauty of Galadriel and Lothlórien, and they learn to respect each other in a rich way. In books three and five, they carry on a friendly contest to see which of them will kill the most Orcs. Later, when they glimpse the caves of Helm's Deep and the forest of Fangorn, they agree that, if they survive the War of the Ring, they will visit these places together and learn to see them through each other's eyes.

Rest Stops

Like all pilgrims in literature and in life, the Fellowship is provided with rest stations along the way. The time they spend in Rivendell and Lothlórien refreshes their bodies and souls and strengthens them for the journey. In both havens of the Elves, they encounter a world where time seems to stand still, and the most ordinary things are filled with magic. Here is how Frodo reacts to both places:

> ". . . it seemed to him that he had stepped over a bridge of time into a corner of the Elder Days, and was now walking in a world that was no more. In Rivendell there was memory of ancient things; in Lórien the ancient things still lived on in the waking world. Evil had been seen and heard there, sorrow had been known; the Elves feared and distrusted the world outside: wolves were howling on the wood's borders: but on the land of Lórien no shadow lay" (II.6).

Lórien is Eden before the Fall, the land of eternal youth that we all yearn for. Being there is like living in a song. Frodo and Sam understand that the Elves are like Hobbits in that they identify fully with their land, but in a much deeper way. When Frodo touches a tree, he feels connected with it, as if he were inside it. Time passes there, but it does not decay.

Still, for Men and Hobbits, Rivendell and Lothlórien can only offer a temporary shelter from mortality. We were not made for immortality and are not bound to the earth the way that the Elves are. The Elves endure, but they lack joy and final hope. That is why the mood in Rivendell and even more Lothlórien is melancholy, elegiac, and poignant. The perpetual spring is really a perpetual autumn. As Galadriel explains to Frodo:

> "Do you not see now wherefore your coming is to us as the footstep of Doom? For if you fail, then we are laid bare to the Enemy. Yet if you succeed, then our power is diminished, and Lothlórien will fade, and the tides of Time will sweep it away. We must depart into the West, or dwindle to a rustic folk of dell and cave, slowly to forget and to be forgotten" (II.7).

Boromir and Sauron

Even before Boromir tries to steal the Ring from Frodo, he makes it clear at the Council of Elrond that he thinks it folly not to use the Ring to protect Gondor from Mordor. He never fully grasps that the Ring always corrupts its owner and cannot be used. The arguments he makes to Frodo to give him the Ring have the appearance of logic and reason, but they lead to his ruin and destruction: "There is a way that seemeth right unto a man, but the end thereof are the ways of death" (Proverbs 16:25; KJV).

In the opening chapter of book three, Aragorn will find Boromir on his deathbed, shot through with Orc arrows. This is significant, because it links Boromir to Isildur who also succumbed to lust for the Ring and was killed by Orc arrows. Boromir, however, finds redemption before he dies, for he gives his life to protect Merry and Pippin from the Orcs and confesses his sin to Aragorn. He gains tragic knowledge and dies in peace.

Sauron will never gain such knowledge. In fact, the only reason that the plan of sending Frodo to Mordor to destroy the Ring works is because Sauron is so blind in his evil that he cannot fathom that

someone in possession of the Ring would
willingly destroy it rather than use it to
rule. Evil cannot finally defeat good;
it cannot even understand it. That is
because evil is not a positive thing
but a corruption of good. One of
the running themes in Tolkien's epic
is that nothing is evil in the beginning—not even Sauron or Morgoth.

THIRTEEN

The Lord of the Rings III:
The Riders of Rohan

Merry and **Pippin** are captured by the **Uruk-Hai**, who take
them to **Saruman**.
Aragorn, **Gimli**, and **Legolas** pursue the Uruk-Hai on foot;
They meet the Riders of Rohan, led by **Éomer**, nephew to
Théoden, King of Rohan.
Éomer's Rohirrim had killed the Uruk-Hai, allowing Merry
and Pippin to escape
Into Fangorn Forest, where they had met **Treebeard** the Ent
and told him about Saruman.
Aragorn, Gimli, and Legolas meet **Gandalf the White** sent
back from death;
The four go to Rohan and find Théoden, whose son
Théodred was killed by Orcs,
Under the spell of **Wormtongue**, whom Saruman had sent to
corrupt Théoden.
Wormtongue seeks to control Rohan and seize **Éowyn**, sister
of Éomer, for his wife.
Gandalf frees Théoden, who leads a victorious battle against
Saruman at Helm's Deep.
Treebeard and the Ents march on Isengard and lay it waste.
Gandalf gives Saruman the chance to repent, but he refuses
and has his staff broken.
After Pippin looks into the palantír thrown at them by
Wormtongue,
Gandalf gives the stone to Aragorn and takes Pippin with
him to Gondor.

THE TALE

Aragorn discovered a dying Boromir pierced by Orc arrows. He had received his wounds defending Merry and Pippin from a troop of Uruk-Hai, a new form of Orc that had been bred by Saruman in Isengard to be able to run and fight in the daylight.

The Hobbits were captured by the Uruk-Hai but not killed because Saruman had ordered his troops to bring to him, unspoiled, any Hobbits they met. Saruman hoped by doing so to acquire the Ring from Frodo. He did not know that Frodo, together with Sam, was on his way to Mordor.

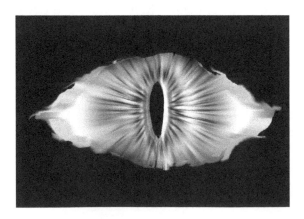

Gimli, Legolas, and Aragorn mourned the fallen Boromir and gave him a "Viking" funeral by putting his body in a boat and floating it down the Anduin.

They then set out on foot to overtake the Uruk-Hai and rescue Merry and Pippin. As they ran across the grassy plains of Rohan, they came upon a regiment of mounted Rohirrim led by Éomer, nephew to Théoden, King of Rohan, and brother to the shield maiden Éowyn.

Aragorn revealed himself to Éomer as the heir of Isildur and told him of the kidnapped Hobbits and of their time in Lothlórien. Éomer was amazed by these tales and wonders and allowed them to take two horses whose riders had died—but with the understanding that they would return them to Théoden in Meduseld, the Golden Mead Hall of Edoras, the capital of Rohan. Éomer further told them that they had recently killed a company of Orcs but saw no Hobbits among the slain. Aragorn, Gimli, and Legolas left to investigate.

Merry and Pippin had been with the Orcs that had been killed by the Rohirrim, but they had escaped into Fangorn Forest. There they met with the Ent Treebeard, a herder of the trees who could speak and move. The Hobbits warned him of the threat of Saruman, who had been cutting down trees to fuel the fires of Orthanc, and the Ents were roused to action. They marched to Isengard to deal with Saruman, knowing they might not return.

Meanwhile, Aragorn, Gimli, and Legolas, though they entered Fangorn too late to see Merry and Pippin, came upon a figure they thought was Saruman. Instead, it turned out to be Gandalf sent back from the dead by Ilúvatar to finish his task of assisting the free peoples of Middle-earth. He was now Gandalf the White, for he was what Saruman could have been had he not been corrupted by Sauron, the Ring, and the palantír.

The four then rode together to Edoras where Théoden had been corrupted himself by Wormtongue, a counselor sent by Saruman to poison Théoden's mind. In mourning over the death of his son Théodred, who had been slain by Orcs, Théoden proved an easy prey to Wormtongue's lies. Like Maeglin, Wormtongue hoped by betraying Théoden to Saruman, he would win control of Edoras and be given princess Éowyn as his wife.

But Gandalf used his powers to free Théoden from the control of Saruman and to send Wormtongue back to his master at Isengard. Théoden then gathered his people and led them to the fortress of Helm's Deep where they would be safe from the attacking forces of

Saruman. There a bitter battle was fought, but the tide turned when Gandalf arrived just in time with reinforcements, and the Ents, along with the wilder, more treeish Huorns, destroyed Isengard and trampled down Saruman's Orc armies.

Gandalf, Aragorn, Gimli, Legolas, Théoden, and Éomer then rode to Isengard where they found Merry and Pippin safe, Isengard flooded, and Saruman and Wormtongue trapped in the tower of Orthanc. Saruman attempted to use his deceitful voice to snare Théoden again and to convince Gandalf to join him, but neither of them were fooled. Gandalf gave Saruman another chance to repent; when he refused again, Gandalf used his now superior magic to break Saruman's staff and expel him from the order of wizards.

In anger, Wormtongue threw Saruman's palantír off the tower at Gandalf.

Gandalf was not hurt, but, the next night, Pippin foolishly stole the palantír from Gandalf's sleeping arms and looked into it. When he did, he was caught by Sauron who tried to control him through the seeing stone. Gandalf rescued Pippin before he could be corrupted and gave the stone to its rightful owner, Aragorn, heir of Isildur. Pippin's folly turned out to be for-tuitous, for it confused Sauron into thinking that Frodo was now a prisoner at Isengard.

CHUCK

To keep Pippin safe, Gandalf took him

on his swift horse, Shadowfax, and rode with him to Gondor to warn Denethor of the coming danger to all of Middle-earth.

DIGGING DEEPER

Narrative Structure

The Lord of the Rings employs a narrative structure that goes back to Homer's *Odyssey*. In *Odyssey*, books one to four, which focus solely on Telemachus, and books five to eight, which focus solely on Odysseus, recount simultaneous action. In Tolkien, book three, which focuses solely on Aragorn, Gimli, Legolas, Gandalf, Merry, and Pippin, and book four, which focuses solely on Frodo and Sam, also recount simultaneous action. The same structure is repeated in books five and six. Within book three, Tolkien uses the same structure to parallel the adventures of Aragorn, Gimli, and Legolas with those of Merry and Pippin.

To help readers hold together the simultaneous action, Tolkien included a chronology in his appendices which details the timing of the parallel events. By consulting this helpful chronology, readers will also learn that Sam and Faramir are both thirty-five, Boromir is forty, Éomer and Eowyn are twenty-seven and twenty-two, Théoden is seventy, Denethor is eighty-eight, and Aragorn is eighty-seven. Readers will further learn that the Fellowship set out from Rivendell on December 25 and that the Ring and Sauron were destroyed on March 25, Annunciation Day for Christians.

The Rohirrim

Tolkien patterned the Riders of Rohan, or Rohirrim, after the Anglo-Saxons of *Beowulf*, though he made them perfect warriors by giving them horses to fight from. They possess great courage linked to a kind of primal innocence that takes joy in riding and battle but can be a bit suspicious of strangers and things beyond their ken. They are the middle men of Middle-earth, far nobler than the wild men whom Sauron and Saruman were able to corrupt, but not as wise or lofty as the Númenóreans of Gondor or the Rangers.

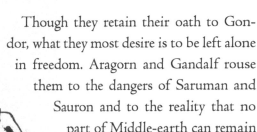

Though they retain their oath to Gondor, what they most desire is to be left alone in freedom. Aragorn and Gandalf rouse them to the dangers of Saruman and Sauron and to the reality that no part of Middle-earth can remain neutral. In a key exchange, Éomer expresses child-like wonder at the marvels he is seeing and is given counsel by Aragorn.

"The world is all grown strange. Elf and Dwarf in company walk in our daily fields; and folk speak with the Lady of the Wood and yet live; and the Sword comes back to war that was broken in the long ages ere the fathers of our fathers rode into the Mark! How shall a man judge what to do in such times?"

"As he ever has judged," said Aragorn. "Good and ill have not changed since yesteryear; nor are they one thing among Elves and Dwarves and another among Men. It is a man's part to discern them, as much in the Golden Wood as in his own house" (III.2).

Éomer senses that something apocalyptic is about to happen but finds it difficult to know how one is to decide or act in such confusing times. Aragorn asserts Tolkien's belief in absolute standards of good and evil, right and wrong. Truth is not culturally relative, nor does it shift from one era to the next. Éomer receives the advice, for he is a man of integrity who does not lie and therefore recognizes intuitively that Aragorn speaks truly.

Treebeard and Saruman

Just as Tolkien rejected the postmodern view of truth as inherently relative, so he rejected the postmodern view of language as possessing no fixed meaning beyond the man-made linguistic structures they are part of. For the Ents, words are tangible and incarnational; they are living things with their own history. Words are not mere signifiers, but names that capture the essence of what they name. When Treebeard meets Merry and Pippin, he works with them to find a place for Hobbits on his list of the names of all creatures.

Like the Elves, who helped to wake up the Trees, the Ents live in unity with nature, and so their magic is equally deep and sympathetic. When Merry and Pippin drink the cool, rich Ent water, it makes them grow taller! When the Ents destroy Isengard, they do so by means of a natural process that has been sped up rather than broken or perverted. Given enough time, tree roots will eat through the concrete slab of a building; Treebeard tears apart Isengard by accelerating that process a hundredfold.

Saruman once respected nature and cared for it, until he embraced the instrumental magic of Sauron. Treebeard explains that Saruman used to walk through Fangorn and ask him questions, but that his face has now become "like windows in a stone wall: windows with shutters inside." He then explains what he thinks has happened to Saruman: "He is plotting to become a Power. He has a mind of metal and wheels; and he does not care for growing things, except as far as they serve him for the moment" (III.4).

Saruman has brought the Industrial Revolution to Isengard, cutting down trees to feed the fires of his munitions factory and his breeding experiments. He even invents a kind of dynamite to blow open a hole in the wall of Helm's Deep. It was this kind of force that laid waste the English countryside Tolkien so loved and swept people away from nature to be cooped up in cities. Saruman threatens the green, Anglo-Saxon innocence of Rohan.

Gandalf, Wormtongue, and Saruman

Gandalf the White is David to Saruman's Saul. God would have established Saul's kingship forever, but, when Saul sinned, the kingship was taken away from him and given to David and his descendants. Gandalf becomes as well the White Rider, mightier than all of the Black Riders. Ilúvatar sent him back from the dead to finish his task, which will not be complete until Sauron is destroyed, and the Fourth Age of Men can begin.

Wormtongue is described as a snake with heavy lidded eyes and (metaphorically) a forked tongue. His chief weapon is to drive Théoden to despair and make him suspicious of his niece and nephew. He is truly the serpent in the innocent Eden of Rohan. Gandalf does not reason with him but rebukes him, as Jesus does the devils he exorcises.

Saruman rejects Gandalf's offer of mercy because, like Sauron, he has embraced utter cynicism, thinking all people are as power-hungry as he is. For one moment, Saruman hesitates and almost accepts Gandalf's offer, but he quickly hardens his heart again. Conviction does not lead to shame and repentance but anger and pride at being exposed.

> "A shadow passed over Saruman's face; then it went deathly white.
> Before he could conceal it, they saw through the mask the anguish
> of a mind in doubt, loathing to stay and dreading to leave its refuge.
> For a second he hesitated, and no one breathed. Then he spoke, and
> his voice was shrill and cold. Pride and hate were conquering him"
> (III.10).

FOURTEEN

The Lord of the Rings IV:
The Road to Mordor

❂

Frodo and Sam make their way through the Emyn Muil
toward Mordor;
They capture Gollum who swears by the Ring to serve them;
He leads them safely through the Dead Marshes to the
Black Gate of Mordor,
But he convinces them to go south through Ithilien for a
safer entryway.
There, they are caught by Faramir, brother of Boromir and
son of Denethor,
And taken to the headquarters of the Rangers of the south,
Henneth Annûn.
Faramir does not steal the Ring but allows them to leave
with Gollum as guide.
Gollum takes them behind Minas Morgul and up a long stair
to a tunnel;
In the tunnel, Frodo is stabbed by Shelob the spider, and
Sam takes the Ring.
Orcs carry Frodo, who is alive, to the Tower of Cirith Ungol;
Sam follows.

❂

THE TALE

In order to make their way to Mordor, Frodo and Sam, after crossing
to the eastern shore of the Anduin, were forced to travel through the

Emyn Muil, a range of barren, jagged rocks and twisting, featureless gullies. It was there that they met with Gollum, who had been following the Fellowship since their journey through the Mines of Moria. When the company had divided, he had followed Frodo, for Frodo had the Ring Gollum desired.

Frodo and Sam captured Gollum, and Frodo made him swear by the Ring that he would obey Frodo. At first they had tied his ankle with elvish rope, but they released him after he complained it hurt him, as did the sun and the moon. They also found he could not eat the lembas. Gollum led them out of the Emyn Muil and then led them by a safe, secret route through the Dead Marshes. Gollum held true to the oath he had taken, but Sam overhead him having an inner-dialogue with his darker side that lusted for the Ring.

As he had promised, Gollum led Frodo and Sam to the Black Gate that led into Mordor, and Frodo told Gollum he could now leave them. But Gollum begged them not to go that way. Instead, he promised to lead them to a safer entryway into Mordor far to the south. They agreed, and he led them through Ithilien, the garden area of Gondor. The smell of flowers and herbs filled Frodo and Sam with hope and life, but Gollum hated the smell.

Not that way, preciousesss. This way.

There Frodo and Sam were captured by Faramir, brother of Boromir and son of Denethor, Steward of Gondor, who was engaged in a war with the evil men who had been corrupted by Sauron. Faramir was the head of the Rangers of the south who guarded the area east of the Anduin from the allies of Mordor. Faramir questioned Frodo and Sam about their journey and about Gollum, who had slipped away, but Frodo told him little.

Faramir led them, blindfolded, to Henneth Annûn, the Window on the West, the secret headquarters of the Rangers. They learned he was Boromir's brother and that he had seen his body floating down the Anduin. As Faramir interrogated them further, Sam slipped up and revealed that they had the Ring. But Faramir was nobler and more prudent than his brother, a man who longed for Númenor and the golden days of Gondor. He told them he would not take the Ring if he found it lying on the road. He understood its danger.

At night, Faramir took Frodo to a waterfall with a pool at its base, where he pointed out Gollum. Frodo begged him not to kill Gollum and told him that Gollum was their guide. Against his better judgment, Faramir allowed the Hobbits to leave with Gollum, though he warned them not to trust Gollum or the route he planned to take them by.

That route took them south to the crossroads east of Osgiliath, then east to Minas Morgul, which, as they passed, sent forth an army to attack Gondor. Behind Minas Morgul was a long, steep, winding stairway up the side of the mountain. At the top of the stair, they had to pass through a tunnel that led into Mordor, which was guarded by the Tower of Cirith Ungol ("pass of the spider"). In the tunnel lived the spider Shelob, daughter of Ungoliant. Gollum planned to have Shelob kill them, so he could take the Ring from Frodo's body.

Frodo blinded the giant spider with the Phial Galadriel had given him, but Shelob still managed to sting him. Sam rushed to the rescue, stabbing one of her eyes, cutting off one of her claws, and getting her to fall on his sword. When Shelob retreated in pain, Sam, thinking Frodo was dead, took the Ring so he could complete the mission. But Frodo was not dead, only stunned by Shelob, who would have cocooned him and fed on his live blood. A group of Orcs carried off Frodo, and Sam followed them to the Tower.

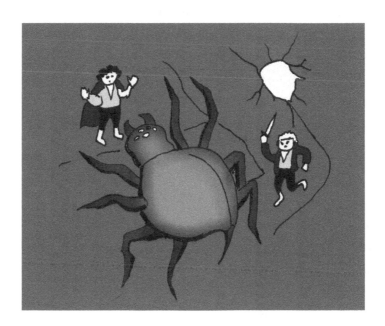

DIGGING DEEPER

Gollum

Just as vampires are "allergic" to all things that are good or holy (light, holy water, the consecrated host from the mass, the cross), so Gollum hates all forms of light and life and anything that has been touched by the "sacred" Elves. That is why the elvish rope burns his skin, and why lembas tastes like dust and ashes to him. Likewise, he hides himself away from the sun and moon—which he calls the Yellow Face and the White Face—and coughs when he breathes in the smell of herbs. He is truly an outcast from hope and joy.

The Ring has the same corrupting influence on the Nazgûl, turning them into vampires who are exposed by light and who dwell in a middle state between life and death. They are, like vampires, the walking dead, cut off from all human community. Gollum and the Nazgûl are like Cain, whose taboo slaying of his brother Abel forces him to live as an enemy to all; his mark will not let him be killed, but he is a lonely wanderer (Genesis 4).

Gollum loves and hates the Ring as he loves and hates light and warmth. His lust for the Ring has robbed him of his "humanity." And yet, a spark of that humanity still remains, surfacing in the inner dialogues he has between Sméagol (his true self) and Gollum (his corrupted self). When he serves Frodo obediently, more of Sméagol comes out, but, when he feels betrayed by Frodo, who turns him over to Faramir as a way of saving his life at the pool, his darker side begins to reemerge again. Evil crushes what little good is left.

Still, Tolkien provides Gollum with a brief flicker of hope, a redemptive moment that almost brings him back to his true self. Shortly before they enter the cave of Shelob, Gollum comes upon Sam and Frodo sleeping, with Frodo's head cradled in Sam's lap. The deep friendship of Sam and Frodo reawakens something in Gollum's heart and:

. . . slowly putting out a trembling hand, very cautiously he touched Frodo's knee—but almost the touch was a caress. For a fleeting moment, could one of the sleepers have seen him, they would have thought that they beheld an old weary hobbit, shrunken by the years that had carried him far beyond his time, beyond friends and kin, and the fields and streams of youth, an old starved pitiable thing (IV.8).

Sadly, the moment is lost when Sam wakes up suddenly and accuses Gollum of sneaking. Immediately, Gollum closes up again and takes to himself the name of sneak. The Ring, whose possession he began with murder, has sucked him dry, robbing him of his self.

Sam and Stories

Speaking of Sam, his interaction here with Gollum shows both his strengths and his weaknesses. His loyalty to Frodo anchors the entire epic, but he is still a provincial Hobbit given to suspicion and xenophobia. Only at the very end, after he has carried the Ring, does he feel some pity for Gollum. He looks up to Frodo with love, respect, and even some reverence, but he does sometimes think that his master is too naïve.

As Frodo embodies the Christian virtue of love (or charity), and Merry and Pippin do that of faith, so Sam is the very incarnation of hope. Nothing can dampen his spirits or crush his indomitable confidence that they will survive and return to the Shire. He even brings his pots and pans with him into Mordor in case they find ingredients for a nice stew! The famous British WWII motto, "Keep Calm and Carry On," appeared in 1939 as Tolkien was beginning his epic; Sam lives out that motto for himself and for Frodo.

Sam also gives one of the most important speeches in *The Lord of the Rings*, one that shows his ability to step back and get perspective on their quest. He realizes in a flash of insight that they are part of the same story that began with Beren and Lúthien and the Silmarils, the light of which still shines in Galadriel's Phial. He realizes, too, that there are two different kinds of tales—there and back again tales like Bilbo goes on in *The Hobbit*; darker tales where the end may not be good—and that the latter are more vital:

> "The brave things in the old tales and songs, Mr. Frodo: adventures, as I used to call them. I used to think that they were things the wonderful folk of the stories went out and looked for, because they wanted them, because they were exciting and life was a bit dull, a kind of sport, as you might say. But that's not the way of it with the tales that really mattered, or the ones that stay in the mind. Folk seem to have been just landed in them, usually—their paths were laid that way, as you put it. But I expect they had lots of chances, like us, of turning back, only they didn't. And if they had, we shouldn't know, because they'd have been forgotten. We hear about those as just went on—and not all to a good end, mind you, at least not to what folk inside a story and not outside it call a good end. You know, coming home, and finding things all right, though not quite the same—like old Mr. Bilbo. But those aren't always the best tales to hear, though they may be the best tales to get landed in! I wonder what sort of a tale we've fallen into?" (IV.8).

Sam is a simple Hobbit, but the maturity and insight he demonstrates in this speech lift him up to the status of a philosopher and sage. The tales that really matter are sometimes more fun to read about than to be a part of. Indeed, it is hard to live one's life in the middle of a tale whose end is uncertain, as so many of us must do. *The Lord of the Rings* is no escapist fairy tale where everyone lives happily ever after. The stakes are very high.

Incidentally, Sam ends his discussion of stories with an observation that borders on the

postmodern. He wonders whether Gollum thinks he is the villain or the hero of the story!

Shelob

When Romantic poets William Blake and Percy Bysshe Shelley argued that Satan was the true hero of *Paradise Lost*, they were both wrong and right. Milton does not present Satan as the hero of his epic, and yet, he depicts his fallen angel in such an energetic and charismatic way that he does threaten to make evil and sin appealing.

Tolkien never falls into that trap. His villains are wholly unappealing, showing forth in their external form and manner the cancer of sin that is eating them from within. True, Saruman retains the lure of his voice, but when Gandalf exposes him, his true ugliness quickly surfaces. Morgoth and Sauron, Orcs and Balrogs, Gollum and the Nazgûl can fool no one as to the corrupted state of their soul.

But, when it comes to Shelob, Tolkien outdoes himself in his depiction of the true nature of evil: anti-life, anti-joy, anti-hope. Shelob does not even seek power as Sauron does. She just devours all that comes in her path, spreading her darkness and fouling all that is good or happy or beautiful. She is utterly bloated and self-absorbed, insatiable in her hunger but feeling neither satisfaction nor satiation nor gratitude. It should come as no surprise that Gollum worships her as an idol of darkness and power.

Faramir

Faramir is one of the noblest characters
in the epic. He alone understands
how the Men of Gondor fell
prey to the same temptation as
the Númenóreans of old: seeking to live forever and building
Egyptian-like monuments to themselves and the dead. He realizes, as his
brother Boromir does not, that the Ring is
altogether evil and will possess anyone who tries
to possess it. He recognizes the peril and has the
courage to flee from it.

Faramir has been trained by Gandalf and has studied
the records of the past, so he can make prudent decisions. He
is a strong warrior, but he does not kill needlessly. Tolkien most identified with Faramir, who gives voice, I believe, to Tolkien's view of war:

> "I would see the White Tree in flower again in the courts of the
> kings, and the Silver Crown return, and Minas Tirith in peace:
> Minas Anor again as of old, full of light, high and fair, beautiful as
> a queen among other queens: not a mistress of many slaves, nay, not
> even a kind mistress of willing slaves. War must be, while we defend
> our lives against a destroyer who would devour all; but I do not love
> the bright sword for its sharpness, nor the arrow for its swiftness, nor
> the warrior for his glory. I love only that which they defend: the city
> of the Men of Númenor; and I would have her loved for her memory,
> her ancientry, her beauty, and her present wisdom. Not feared, save as
> men may fear the dignity of a man, old and wise" (IV.5).

Although Tolkien thought the stories of King Arthur had been too
corrupted by French influence to represent an authentic native mythology for England, Faramir speaks here as a knight of the Round Table.
His vision for Gondor-Camelot is of a place where might is used for

right and where the wisdom of age (think Merlin as well as Gandalf) is honored more highly than the power of the sword (think Gawain as well as Denethor/Boromir). War is not to be sought as an end in itself but as a vehicle for preserving true justice.

Faramir is a dreamer and an idealist, but he is neither weak nor foolish nor cowardly. He knows that the Ring might make Gondor powerful, but it would do so by transforming Gondor into an evil kingdom like Mordor. For Faramir, the ends do not justify the means.

Faramir is also something of a mystic who understands spiritual things. He will not speak again of the Ring or name Sauron. He gives sound advice but does not presume to judge. He knows that if he brings the Ring to his father, he will gain his love and approval, but he will not perform an evil deed to win the paternal affection that has been denied him.

FIFTEEN

The Lord of the Rings V:
Defending Gondor

⚙

Gandalf and **Pippin** arrive at Minas Tirith; Pippin pledges
  service to **Denethor**.

Merry pledges service to **Théoden**, who answers Gondor's
  call for aid.

Aragorn, **Legolas**, and **Gimli** take the Paths of the Dead to
  meet the **Oathbreakers**.

Aragorn frees them from the curse of **Isildur** after they help
  him defeat the corsairs;

Aragorn seizes their ships and sails with them up the
  Anduin to rescue Gondor.

Éowyn and Merry accompany the Rohirrim in disguise as
  they ride to Minas Tirith.

Faramir is injured trying to retake Osgiliath, and the Orc
  army marches to Gondor.

A great battle is fought on the Pelennor Fields, where
  Théoden is slain,

But Merry and Éowyn defeat his killer, the Lord of the Nazgûl.

Denethor, driven to despair by what he sees in his palantír,
  kills himself;

He tries to take Faramir with him, but Gandalf and Pippin
  rescue him.

While Faramir, Éowyn, and Merry recover in the Houses of
  Healing,

Aragorn, Gandalf, Legolas, Gimli, and Pippin march to the
  Black Gates;

They hope to draw out the armies of Mordor to give **Frodo**
  and **Sam** a fighting chance.

⚙

THE TALE

When Gandalf and Pippin arrived in Minas Tirith, they were quickly ushered into the presence of Denethor, Steward of Gondor. Denethor questioned Pippin sharply about the death of his son Boromir, and Pippin, in a surge of compassion and honor, took a pledge to serve Denethor out of gratitude for Boromir having saved his life and that of Merry.

Meanwhile, as Pippin swore his oath to serve Denethor, Merry, deep in the heart of Rohan, offered his own hand in service to Théoden. Soon, the Rohirrim would ride southeast for Minas Tirith, answering the beacons lit by Gondor to signal to Rohan that she needed her aid in war. Merry would accompany them in secret.

But Aragorn would take a different path in fulfillment of his own destiny, one that would take him south through the winding caverns of the White Mountains. There dwelt the ghosts of the Oathbreakers, who, tempted by Sauron, had forsaken their pledge to fight alongside Isildur at the end of the Second Age and been cursed by him to a living death.

Although the cave of the Oathbreakers terrified all who came near, Aragorn, for the sake of Middle-earth, braved the Paths of the Dead, accompanied by Legolas, Gimli, and a group of northern Rangers led by Elrond's sons Elladan and Elrohir. Aragorn, heir of Isildur, swore to release them from their oath if they helped him to defeat Sauron.

Now, a group of evil southern Men had gathered their pirate ships along the Anduin to sail north and meet up with the forces of Mordor. Knowing such a combined force would overwhelm Gondor, Aragorn compelled the Oathbreakers to follow him as he rode to the southern shore of the Anduin. There, the numinous dread of the ghosts caused the pirates to flee in terror. Aragorn and company seized the boats and freed the slaves of the corsairs; then, Aragorn released the dead from Isildur's three-thousand-year-old curse.

Éowyn had accepted Aragorn's refusal to allow her to accompany him along the Paths of the Dead, but when her uncle Théoden also forbad her to join the Rohirrim as they rode to Minas Tirith, she disguised herself as a man and joined them in secret. She took with her on her horse Merry, who had also been forbidden by Théoden to come.

Meanwhile, back in Gondor, Denethor criticized his son Faramir for not bringing him the Ring, then shamed him into riding out on a suicide mission to take back Osgiliath. The ruined city had fallen to the Orc army, which had ridden out of Minas Morgul led by the Lord of the Nazgûl. Along with the other Ring-wraiths, he rode now upon a foul, winged beast bred by Sauron. The mission was a failure, and Faramir was carried back half dead.

So commenced the Battle of the Pelennor Fields in the plain outside the city. Gondor would surely have perished had she not been saved by the sudden and serendipitous appearance of the Riders of Rohan from the west and the ships of the corsairs, now controlled by Aragorn and company, from the east. She was saved as well by the brave slaying of the Lord of the Nazgûl. It had been prophesied that no living man could slay him; the female Éowyn and the Hobbit Merry killed him and his foul steed.

In the midst of triumph, the Rohirrim mourned the death of Théoden, and Éowyn and Merry, deeply injured by the Nazgûl, were taken to the Houses of Healing. As for Faramir, Denethor, convinced his son was dead and the race of Men about to fall, lit a mighty pyre, intending to immolate himself and Faramir upon it. Gandalf and Pippin rescued Faramir, but Denethor refused to go on living and threw himself into the fire.

Like Saruman, Denethor had discovered a palantír through which Sauron had caused him to despair. Because the palantír had shown him the black sails of the corsairs sailing up the Anduin, he had believed Gondor would fall. What he did not know was that the ships were led by Aragorn, the heir of Isildur whose return had long been awaited but which he, in his pride, had refused to acknowledge. He would rather die than give up his power.

Aragorn, the messianic king, used his power to draw Éowyn, Faramir, and Merry out of the darkness and back into the light. As they slowly healed, Éowyn and Faramir came to know and love each other. Meanwhile, Aragorn, Gandalf, Legolas, Gimli, Pippin, and the survivors of the Pelennor Fields marched to the Black Gates to challenge Sauron directly. Though they knew they had no chance of winning, they hoped to empty out Mordor and thus buy Frodo and Sam the chance to get the Ring to Mount Doom.

DIGGING DEEPER

Denethor and Théoden

When we first meet Denethor and Théoden, they are quite similar. Both are old, widowed kings of Men who have just lost their beloved son (Boromir and Théodred) and have given themselves over to despair. That despair allows Sauron (by means of the palantír) and Saruman (by means of Wormtongue) to manipulate and control them so that they initially cut themselves off from their closest kin (the former from his son Faramir; the latter from his niece and nephew Éowyn and Éomer) and refuse the advice of Gandalf.

Each is served by a loyal Hobbit (Denethor by Pippin; Théoden by Merry) who acts as a sort of court jester who tries to lift his spirits while acting as a surrogate son. Each feels overwhelmed by the forces arrayed against him and must lead his people through the desperate battles of Helm's Deep and the Pelennor Fields. Here, however, the similarities cease, and the differences emerge.

Whereas Théoden is, quite literally, exorcised by Gandalf and throws off the poisonous control of Wormtongue and Saruman, Denethor slips further and further into the despair and paranoia brought on by his misuse of the palantír. In the end, Théoden dies a hero's death in the Battle of Pelennor Fields, exclaiming triumphantly as he dies that he will not be ashamed to sit beside his fathers in the afterlife. Denethor, in sharp contrast, dies as a suicide, clutching in his hands the very palantír that has corrupted him.

"And it was said that ever after, if any man looked in that Stone, unless he had a great strength of will to turn it to other purpose, he saw only two aged hands withering in flame" (V.7).

That memorable image of the withered hands of Denethor captures perfectly what happens to the human soul when it refuses to let go of pride and despair. While Théoden, once freed from Wormtongue, allows himself to be aided by Aragorn as well as Éowyn and Éomer, Denethor scorns the assistance of both Gandalf and Faramir. He even accuses his son of being a wizard's pupil and of heeding Gandalf rather than himself. Although Gandalf explains to Denethor that both of them have been appointed stewards of Middle-earth, Denethor resists the messianic return of Aragorn, the true king of Gondor:

> "But I say to thee, Gandalf Mithrandir, I will not be thy tool! I am Steward of the House of Anárion. I will not step down to be the dotard chamberlain of an upstart. Even were his claim proved to me, still he comes but of the line of Isildur. I will not bow to such a one, last of a ragged house long bereft of lordship and dignity" (V.7).

Like Saruman, Denethor sees Gandalf as a threat and a rival, rather than a wise counselor who wishes to set him free from his own self-destructive pride. Neither Saruman nor Denethor knows the joy of surrender and obedience. They will never say what John the Baptist says of Christ: "He must increase, but I must decrease" (John 3:30; KJV).

Both Éowyn and Faramir end up in the Houses of Healing but for very different reasons. Éowyn is injured by the Lord of the Nazgûl when she steps forward to protect her uncle Théoden, who has himself been mortally wounded by the Witch King. Faramir is injured, first because his father vindictively sends him on the suicide mission to retake Osgiliath, and second because Denethor tries to burn him on the pyre. Still, both survive and heal the wounds and bad decisions of their uncle/father by falling in love and uniting the Men of Rohan and Gondor through their marriage (in book six).

Aragorn and Éowyn

Were *The Lord of the Rings* a typical fantasy novel, Aragorn and Éowyn would fall in love, marry, and rule as king and queen of Middle-earth, but Tolkien's epic and his characters are far more complicated than that.

It is not enough for Aragorn to become king. He is a messianic figure who brings healing, freedom, and rebirth, and who stands at the apex of all the hopes and fears, victories and defeats, struggles and sorrows of Tolkien's legendarium. It is not the shieldmaiden but the Elf maiden whom he must marry, thus bringing to completion and consummation the sacred bloodline that flows through *The Silmarillion*.

To no lesser man than the King of Rohan and Gondor will Elrond give his daughter; for no lesser man than the heir of Thingol and Melian, Beren and Lúthien, and Tuor and Idril will Arwen give her heart and her immortality. Only through this final blending of Man and Elf can the Third Age be brought to an end and the days of the Dominion of Men be ushered in. As a pledge of this great transition, between the crowning of Aragorn and his marriage to Arwen, Gandalf reveals to Aragorn a sapling from the White Tree of Gondor.

Several other messianic events prepare for the great marriage of Aragorn and Arwen, a wedding that clearly points ahead to the marriage of Christ the Lamb (the Bridegroom) and the Church (his Bride) that is celebrated in the closing two chapters of Revelation.

First, when Aragorn seizes the ships from the corsairs, he sets free the slaves who have been working at the oars. Second, he heals, by his kingly touch and his royal presence, the deep wounds of Merry, Éowyn, and Faramir, drawing them out of darkness and back into the light. Third, when he enters Gondor, his true majesty is revealed and the people call him Elfstone, the very messianic title that had been prophesied for him at his birth.

As for Éowyn, Tolkien presents her as a woman of high courage, valor, and loyalty, who yet thinks too much of honor and fears too much that she will be caged by her duties and responsibilities. She loves Aragorn, but her love proves to be an illusion, a desire for renown and glory, as a soldier might feel for a lordly captain. For a time, her infatuation for Aragorn blinds her to the love of her people, of her brother Éomer, and of Faramir.

After she is injured, it is Aragorn who restores her to life, but it is Faramir who helps her to see herself and to understand her heart.

While she fears that Faramir feels only pity for her, Faramir assures her that she is a shieldmaiden of great renown who has committed a great and memorable deed (the slaying of the Witch King) and has won his undying love.

> Then the heart of Éowyn changed, or else at last she understood it. And suddenly her winter passed, and the sun shone on her.
> "I stand in Minas Anor, the Tower of the Sun," she said; "and behold! the Shadow has departed! I will be a shieldmaiden no longer, nor vie with the great Riders, nor take joy only in the songs of slaying. I will be a healer and love all things that grow and are not barren" (VI. 5).

Priest, King, and Prophet

One of the indications that Jesus Christ was the Messiah prophesied in scripture is that he combined in himself three offices that were kept separate in the Old Testament: priest, king, and prophet. Whereas the kingly line of David and the priestly line of Aaron issued from two different tribes (Judah and Levi, respectively), and whereas God used prophets like Isaiah, Ezekiel, Jeremiah, and Nathan to convict his kings when they went astray, Jesus was, at once, the Lion of Judah and Root of David (Revelation 5:5), the high priest who intercedes with his blood (Hebrews 9:11-14), and the prophet who spoke with authority but was often rejected (Luke 4:24, 32).

In the pre-Christian *Lord of the Rings*, Tolkien divides the three offices amongst his three main messianic characters: Gandalf the Prophet, Frodo the Priest, and Aragorn the King. Gandalf shows forth his prophetic office by counseling Théoden, Denethor, and Aragorn and by directing the paths of the Fellowship. Frodo shows forth his priestly office by bearing the weight of the Ring, which itself is an embodiment of sin. Aragorn shows forth his kingly office by returning to Gondor and being crowned as the heir of Isildur.

To drive home these three vital messianic offices, Tolkien cleverly arranges to have all three characters suffer through an experience of death and resurrection. In Gandalf's case, that death is a literal one, when he falls into the pit in the Mines of Moria and is slain by the Balrog that he himself slays. But death cannot hold him, and he is returned to life by Ilúvatar as Gandalf the White so that he can complete his ministry in Middle-earth.

Though the deaths of Frodo and Aragorn are more figurative than literal, they both take place, like the literal death of Gandalf, in a cave. It is in the cave of Shelob that Frodo is stung and falls into a state of paralysis that Sam mistakes for death. From that simulated death, Frodo returns to life in book six to complete the mission assigned to him.

Aragorn also enters a cave when he takes the Paths of the Dead and meets with the Oathbreakers. When he emerges from the cave and leads his company on horseback to the shores of the Anduin, the villagers who watch in terror think Aragorn is as dead as the ghostly army that accompanies him. In some ways, he enters the cave as Aragorn the Ranger but exits as Aragorn the King, ready now to set free the captives on the ships of the corsairs and to fulfill his role as King of Rohan and Gondor and husband of Arwen.

"Prophet"

"Priest"

It is significant that Tolkien identifies the Oathbreakers as the Men of Dunharrow. According to the Apostle's Creed, between Christ's death and resurrection, he harrowed hell—breaking down the doors and rescuing the righteous people of the Old Testament who had been waiting for him in Limbo. By prefiguring Christ's descent into Hades, Aragorn also reflects such epic heroes as Odysseus, Aeneas, and Dante who braved and overcame the numinous fear of the underworld.

SIXTEEN

The Lord of the Rings VI:
The Return of the King

Sam frees **Frodo** from the Tower of Cirith Ungol and gives him back the Ring.

Disguised as Orcs, they make their way to Mount Doom.

When Gollum realizes Frodo means to destroy the Ring, he tries to stop him;

Frodo overcomes Gollum, and Sam almost kills him, but stops out of pity.

Frodo refuses to destroy the Ring and puts it on;

Gollum leaps on the invisible Frodo, bites off the Ring, and falls with it into the fire.

The Eye of **Sauron**, along with the towers of Mordor, are destroyed;

The Eagles save Sam and Frodo from the ruins of Mordor.

Aragorn is crowned, Aragorn weds **Arwen**, and **Faramir** weds **Éowyn**.

Treebeard allows **Saruman** and **Wormtongue** to escape from Orthanc;

They go to the Shire and turn it into an industrialized, totalitarian country.

Sam, Frodo, **Merry**, and **Pippin** return and take back the Shire.

Wormtongue kills Saruman in a fit of rage, and the Hobbits kill Wormtongue.

Frodo, still in pain from his wound at Weathertop, travels to the Grey Havens;

He takes the ship to Valinor, along with **Gandalf**, **Elrond**, **Galadriel**, and **Bilbo**.

THE TALE

Although Sam was briefly tempted to use the Ring for himself, his love for his master kept him focused, and he pushed on to rescue Frodo from the Tower of Cirith Ungol. Using the Phial of Galadriel to blind and overcome the Two Watchers, vulture-headed statues that guarded Mordor, Sam entered the Tower and began to sing a song of hope. The song reached and was echoed by Frodo, and Sam killed the Orc guarding Frodo. The other Orcs killed each other fighting for a priceless mithril coat Bilbo had given Frodo!

Sam returned the Ring to Frodo, and the two, disguised as Orcs, made their way toward Mount Doom. As they proceeded, the burden of the Ring grew heavier, and Frodo became so overwhelmed by its dark power that he lost all memory of food and drink, nature and the heavens, and came even to distrust Sam. In the end, Frodo was so weak that Sam had to carry him to the doorway that led into the central cavern of Mount Doom.

As Frodo prepared to throw the Ring in the fire, Gollum reappeared and tried to stop him. But Frodo overpowered and rebuked him, warning him that he would die if he tried again to take the Ring. As Frodo moved toward the fire, Sam prepared to kill Gollum—but a strange pity welled up in his heart. Sam too had borne the Ring and felt its awful power. Moving beyond his anger, he spared the miserable Gollum and ordered him to leave.

All seemed well until Frodo, standing on the edge of the fiery chasm, cried out that the Ring was his and that he would not destroy it. He then put the Ring on his finger and instantly vanished. Sam gasped in horror but could do nothing to stop Frodo, for, at that moment, Gollum struck him from behind. Gollum

I hasses it!

My finger!

then leapt on the invisible Frodo and bit off his finger.

Now in possession of his precious Ring, Gollum leapt up in victory, tottered for a second on the edge of the chasm, and then fell with the Ring into the fire.

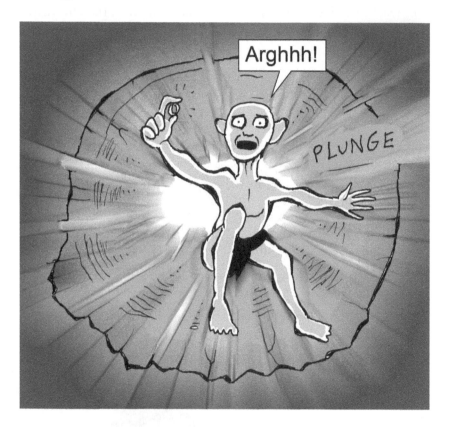

With a roar, the Eye of Sauron, together with the towers and battlements of Mordor, crumbled to dust and were no more. Sam and Frodo sought high ground as lava swirled about them. Even then, they would have perished had not two Eagles, led by Gwaihir and Gandalf, rescued them from the ruins of Mordor.

Thus was Sauron defeated, Aragorn crowned, and the weddings

of Aragorn and Arwen and Faramir and Éowyn celebrated. With the returned king safely on his throne, Middle-earth was restored and set free, but evil yet lingered. Treebeard had been commissioned by Gandalf to keep Saruman and Wormtongue imprisoned in the Tower of Orthanc, but, out of pity, he had let them escape. This had unfortunate consequences, for Saruman used his freedom to enslave the Shire, transforming it into a totalitarian police state.

When Frodo, Sam, Merry, and Pippin returned to the Shire, they discovered that it had been laid waste. The great tree under which Bilbo had celebrated his 111th birthday had been cut down, the gardens dug up, the houses turned to tenements, and the water and air fouled by an industrialized mill. But they were no longer the same Hobbits who had left the Shire the year before. They rallied the good Hobbits, saved the Shire, and set things to right. They offered Saruman mercy, but he refused it and even tried to stab Frodo.

When they offered mercy to Wormtongue, Saruman accused him of murdering one of the Hobbits so that they would not allow him to stay in the Shire. Enraged, Wormtongue stabbed Saruman in the back, and, before Frodo could stop them, the Hobbits killed him. The next year was a golden one in the Shire, but the wound Frodo had received from the Witch King on Weathertop never healed, and he knew he had to leave Middle-earth.

After leaving his estate to Sam and his wife Rose, Frodo went to the Grey Havens, where a ship was leaving Middle-earth for Valinor. Frodo took Arwen's spot on the ship, for she had chosen mortality to marry Aragorn. He bid farewell to Sam, Merry, and Pippin, and sailed away, accompanied by Gandalf, Elrond, Galadriel, and Bilbo.

DIGGING DEEPER

Mordor and the Ring

Though the majority of Tolkien's influences came from ancient and medieval literature, his depiction of Mordor reads like a combination of the prevailing mood of despair and infertility in T. S. Eliot's *The Waste Land*, the valley of ashes in F. Scott Fitzgerald's *The Great Gatsby*, and the external and internal journey into madness and moral ambiguity in Joseph Conrad's *The Heart of Darkness*.

True, the starved, barren landscapes of Mordor reflect the no man's land Tolkien saw in WWI, but they offer a more general commentary on a modern, industrialized, totalitarian world that has laid waste to nature and flattened out humanity, leaving us stranded in a world without hope or joy or promise of new life. As Frodo journeys deeper into the heart of Mordor and the weight of the Ring increases, his personality is consumed:

> "No taste of food, no feel of water, no sound of wind, no memory of tree or grass or flower, no image of moon or star are left to me. I am naked in the dark, Sam, and there is no veil between me and the wheel of fire [the Eye of Sauron]. I begin to see it even with my waking eyes, and all else fades" (VI.3).

Mordor is an anthill where individuality is crushed and all serve the collective. It is a colorless, sexless, classless world where courage, honor, and beauty have no meaning. The Ring does not enhance life; it merely stretches it out until all is dust and ashes.

Readers are shocked every time they reach Mount Doom, and Frodo refuses to destroy the Ring. But they shouldn't be. The Ring embodies human sin and depravity and cannot be destroyed by a simple exertion of free will. What saves Frodo in the end is not his strength or his will power, but the pity that Bilbo, Frodo, and Sam all showed to Gollum.

The Eucatastrophe

In "On Fairy-stories" (see chapter eighteen, below), Tolkien explains that one of the key ingredients of the best fairy tales is that they feature a eucatastrophe, a word that Tolkien coined by joining the Greek prefix "eu" (which means "good") to the word catastrophe. The Fall of Man is a catastrophe, but it is a *good* catastrophe, for it led to the incarnation of Christ. Just so, the eucatastrophe of Good Friday, when Christ was crucified, is Easter Sunday, when he rose from the dead, thus conquering Satan, sin, and death. Behind all eucatastrophes is the mysterious working of God's grace.

The unforgettable eucatastrophe of *The Lord of the Rings* occurs when Frodo's failure to destroy the Ring gives way, by a profound act of grace, to Gollum's stealing of the Ring and his subsequent plunge into Mount Doom. Gandalf had counseled Frodo to show pity to Gollum, for he felt Gollum still had a part to play, for good or ill, in the history of the Ring. Neither Frodo, nor first-time readers, could have guessed that Gollum would be the one responsible for saving the Ring and Frodo's life, but then it is just such unexpected turns that mark all true fairy tales. As Tolkien expresses it in "On Fairy-stories":

> "The consolation of fairy-stories, the joy of the happy ending: or more
> correctly of the good catastrophe, the sudden joyous 'turn' (for there

is no true end to any fairy-tale): this joy, which is one of the things which fairy-stories can produce supremely well, is not essentially 'escapist' nor 'fugitive.' In its fairy-tale—or otherworld—setting, it is a sudden and miraculous grace: never to be counted on to recur. It does not deny the existence of dyscatastrophe, of sorrow and failure: the possibility of these is necessary to the joy of deliverance; it denies (in the face of much evidence, if you will) universal final defeat and in so far is evangelium [good news], giving a fleeting glimpse of Joy, Joy beyond the walls of the world, poignant as grief."

It is the complexity of this consolation, which takes place alongside sorrow and failure, that accounts both for Frodo's inability to destroy the Ring, and for his inability to remain in the Shire. Middle-earth has been saved, but Frodo is too wounded, not only by the Witch King's blade but by Shelob's sting and Gollum's bite, to participate in the happy ending. He must take his three "stigmata" and bear them and himself away to the undying lands of Valinor where he can find healing "beyond the walls of the world." Here is how Frodo explains it to Sam:

"I tried to save the Shire, and it has been saved, but not for me. It must often be so, Sam, when things are in danger: some one has to give them up, lose them, so that others may keep them" (VI.9).

The Scouring of the Shire

WWI was supposed to be the war to end all wars, but it gave birth to thugs, dictators, and totalitarian ideologies of every shape and kind. In the same way, the War of the Ring did not end all evil and intrigue in Middle-earth. Indeed, Saruman could never have gotten a foothold in the Shire had not Frodo's cousin Lotho, consumed with greed, invited him in.

Just as the bourgeois capitalists of 1930s Germany who thought they could manipulate Hitler for their own ends soon discovered that Hitler controlled them, so Lotho finds himself reduced to a figurehead by Saruman and his ruffians. Worse yet, he finds that Saruman's utopia is not to be one of wine, women, and song, but a dystopia marked by urban sprawl, industrial pollution, and economic scarcity. The simple pleasures of beer and pipes and fellowship that Tolkien so loved are proscribed and the pubs shut down.

Tolkien had lived to see his beloved Sarehole fall prey to the long fingers of the Industrial Revolution. He knew that the pastoral tranquility of the Shire was not to be taken for granted but demanded perpetual vigilance and sacrifice. It is significant that Gandalf does not travel to the Shire with the Hobbits. Instead, he assures them that they have matured enough to settle their own affairs without him. Tolkien, I believe, meant Gandalf's words to be a call and a challenge to modern readers as well:

> "I am not coming to the Shire. You must settle its affairs yourselves; that is what you have been trained for. Do you not yet understand? My time is over: it is no longer my task to set things to rights, nor to help folk to do so. And as for you, my dear friends, you will need no help. You are grown up now. Grown indeed very high; among the great you are, and I have no longer any fear at all for any of you" (VI.7).

SEVENTEEN

Tolkien on Beowulf

AS I EXPLAINED IN chapter one, Tolkien's 1936 lecture, *"Beowulf: The Monsters and the Critics,"* revolutionized *Beowulf* studies by forcing scholars who had previously viewed the Anglo-Saxon epic as nothing more than a linguistic-historical artifact to study and enjoy it as a poem, as a work of literary genius that offered timeless insight into the nature of man and mortality, good and evil, heroism and treachery.

But Tolkien's great lecture also offers insights into his own legendarium that can enrich one's experience of *The Silmarillion*, *The Hobbit*, and *The Lord of the Rings*.

First, the Catholic Tolkien's decision to set his tales of Middle-earth in a time before God revealed himself to Abraham bears the direct influence of *Beowulf*. As Tolkien explains in his lecture, the anonymous poet of *Beowulf* was a Christian monk who consciously set his epic in a pre-Christian world. Because of this, we as readers catch glimpses of the greater biblical revelation that is not perceived by the characters.

The hero of the epic, Tolkien explains, "moves in a northern heroic age imagined by a Christian, and therefore has a noble and gentle quality, though conceived to be a pagan." That is why the consolation that the author offers him is not the Christian heaven but the heroic pagan end Beowulf would have desired: "His funeral is not Christian, and his reward is the recognized virtue of his kingship and the hopeless sorrow of his people."

Second, *Beowulf* shares with Tolkien's legendarium an elegiac, melancholy mood, partly because the Christian heaven has not yet been revealed. This mood is felt particularly strongly in the Elves, who know they are fighting a war that can never fully be won. Their combination of quiet regret and stoic courage in the face of ever-present doom is more Norse pagan than Judeo-Christian.

Third, the worlds of *Beowulf* and *The Lord of the Rings* are layered in a similar way. Both are old, old tales that are yet suffused with a sense of an even older period that has been lost in the mists of time. Tolkien describes this unique aspect of the Old English epic in a way that can be directly transferred to his own epic:

> [*Beowulf*] "is now to us itself ancient; and yet its maker was telling of things already old and weighted with regret, and he expended his art in making keen that touch upon the heart which sorrows have that are both poignant and remote. If the funeral of *Beowulf* moved once like the echo of an ancient dirge, far-off and hopeless, it is to us as a memory brought over the hills, an echo of an echo."

In trying to catalogue those layers of history, both Tolkien and the *Beowulf* poet present themselves as editors rather than authors: chroniclers of a heroic age that is no more.

Fourth, the monsters in *Beowulf* (Grendel, Grendel's mother, and the dragon), like the monsters in Tolkien's legendarium (Glaurung and Smaug, Ungoliant and Shelob, the Balrogs and the Orcs, Morgoth and Sauron, and the undead Nazgûl) come as close to pure evil as any figures in literature. They lay waste to the world, not merely so they can gain power, but because they hate life, joy, and hope.

The remorseless, gratuitous nature of their evil lends a moral clarity to *Beowulf* and *The Lord of the Rings* that is missing from much of the literature of the last two centuries. And yet, despite the epic battles between good and evil, light and darkness that animate both epics, there exists a moral ambiguity that haunts many of the characters and gives depth and urgency to their decisions. That ambiguity is expressed in Tolkien through the internal struggles of Boromir, Saruman, Wormtongue, Théoden, Denethor, and Gollum.

Fifth, while both epics are haunted by a deep sense of fatalism and of the unavoidability of destiny, a counter-sense of providence yet hangs over all the proceedings.

Sixth, Heorot, the wonderful Mead-Hall of Hrothgar, King of the

Danes, is directly reflected in Meduseld, the Mead-Hall of Théoden, King of the Rohirrim. Here, as in the Round Table of Camelot, we find joy, brotherhood, generosity, and true courage and honor. The warriors who meet here are brave and strong, yet they feel and love deeply. Their true desire is for peace and fellowship, but they will fight when they must. Here too pacts of loyalty are sworn that hold back the darkness and treachery of the world.

Mead Hall

The Rohirrim, as I mentioned in chapter one, *are* the Anglo-Saxons of *Beowulf,* but Tolkien perfects their warrior skills by giving them horses to ride and fight on!

Seventh, over *Beowulf* and *The Lord of the Rings* there hangs a strong sense of loss and nostalgia. Joy and fellowship are so fleeting, while the darkness is always lurking in the shadows, waiting to break through. In the stunned impotence that Hrothgar feels over the destruction of Heorot by Grendel, we catch a glimpse of Théoden and Denethor, both of whom give up all hope, overpowered by fate and forces of evil that they cannot control.

Near the end of *Beowulf,* in one of the lengthier digressions, we hear of an old man lamenting over the execution of his son and wishing to give up in despair. This grief-stricken, immobilized father could be Théoden or Denethor weeping over Théodred or Boromir. Just as Beowulf helps to revive and restore Hrothgar, so Gandalf exorcises the demons that haunt Théoden and restores him to his throne. Sadly, he is unable to do the same for Denethor, who chooses to remain in his grief and despair.

Eighth, when Beowulf descends into the haunted mere to face Grendel's mother, he must not only overcome his fear of death, but his numinous fear of the unknown dread that awaits him beneath the water. In the same way, when Aragorn takes the Paths of the Dead, he must transcend his own fears of physical death and of the spiritually uncanny.

EIGHTEEN
Tolkien on Fairy Tales

TOLKIEN'S 1939 LECTURE, "On Fairy-stories," later expanded into a 1947 essay, was, in its own modest way, almost as groundbreaking as his *Beowulf* lecture. In it, Tolkien not only defends fairy stories as a legitimate genre meant for child and adult readers alike, but offers multiple perspectives from which to understand and analyze them.

Fantasy, Tolkien argues, is neither anti-science nor anti-reason. It does not hurt or insult our rational faculties but can strengthen and clarify them. In fact, fantasy worlds that are constructed along logical, consistent lines will be better and more artistic than those that are put together haphazardly—as, sadly, Tolkien felt Lewis's Chronicles of Narnia were.

Fantasy is also not inherently sinful or anti-God. Yes, Tolkien concedes, fantasy can:

> "be carried to excess. It can be ill done. It can be put to evil uses. It may even delude the minds out of which it came. But of what human thing in this fallen world is that not true? Men have conceived not only of elves, but they have imagined gods, and worshipped them, even worshipped those most deformed by their authors' own evil. But they have made false gods out of other materials: their notions, their banners, their monies; even their sciences and their social and economic theories have demanded human sacrifice. *Abusus non tollit usum* ["abuse does not take away use"]. Fantasy remains a human right: we make in our measure and in our derivative mode, because we are made: and not only made, but made in the image and likeness of a Maker."

As in *The Lord of the Rings*, evil is not a positive thing, but a perversion of something that was once good. The magical powers Ilúvatar entrusts to Gandalf and Saruman are finally neutral; the difference is that Gandalf uses them for good to protect Middle-earth while Saruman uses them for evil to increase his own power and pride. Fantasy too can be used for good or evil, but then so can money, science, innovative ideas, and the Bible.

The innate desire of fantasy authors to create new worlds is not a sign of sin or pride but an acknowledgment that we were made in the image of a Maker. To embody this idea, Tolkien coined the word "sub-creator" to describe the proper relationship between the maker and the Maker. Here is how Tolkien explains the concept in poetic form:

> "Although now long estranged,
> Man is not wholly lost nor wholly changed.
> Dis-graced he may be, yet is not dethroned,
> and keeps the rags of lordship once he owned:
> Man, Sub-creator, the refracted light
> through whom is splintered from a single White
> to many hues, and endlessly combined
> in living shapes that move from mind to mind.
> Though all the crannies of the world we filled

with Elves and Goblins, though we dared to build
Gods and their houses out of dark and light,
and sowed the seed of dragons, 'twas our right
(used or misused). The right has not decayed.
We make still by the law in which we're made."

In addition to defending the right of religious believers to create fantasy, this poem offers a glimpse into Tolkien's creative process. This is precisely what he "dared" to do in his legendarium, and the world is a better and richer place for it!

Here are some other insights from "On Fairy-stories" that illuminate Tolkien's epic.

- Critics of fantasy accuse it of being escapist, but escapism is not always a bad thing. If I am a political prisoner or a prisoner of war, it is right and proper that I should seek to escape. It is also right and proper that I should not spend all my time thinking and writing about my jailers or the bars of my prison.
- The true sub-creator creates a Secondary World that is like the Primary World but that possesses its own internal

consistency. Such construction often calls for more skill than realistic novels that merely imitate without seeking a greater coherence.

- By provoking awe and wonder toward the Secondary World, the best fantasy empowers its readers to retain that awe and wonder when they return to the Primary World. By so doing, fantasy cleanses our perceptions, allowing us to see our own world afresh, as if for the first time.

- Fantasy restores the potency of words and the power of things.

- Fantasy can include satire, but it must never dismiss or ridicule the magic itself.

- The best fairy tales satisfy our primordial desire to travel to other dimensions of space and time and to commune with living beings unlike those in our own world.

- In our Primary World, magic is a technique used for power. In the Secondary World, it is an enchantment that enriches rather than deludes and dominates.

- The Christian gospel ("good news") of Christ's birth, death, and resurrection does not do away with fairy tales but hallows them. The Christian "story is supreme; and it is true. Art has been verified. God is the Lord, of angels, and of men—and of elves. Legend and History have met and fused."

NINETEEN

Tolkien in Faerie

IN ADDITION TO *The Silmarillion*, *The Hobbit*, and *The Lord of the Rings*, Tolkien wrote a number of shorter pieces that help flesh out his legendarium: a series of letters that he wrote to his children each yuletide about Father Christmas; a number of shorter poems that he collected and published as *The Adventures of Tom Bombadil*; and three short stories that transport their reader to the world of faerie—"Smith of Wootton Major," "Farmer Giles of Ham," and "Leaf By Niggle."

Letters from Father Christmas

Beginning in 1920 and ending in 1943, Tolkien sent yearly letters from Father Nicholas Christmas to his children. The letters made use of various scripts and designs (including cave drawings), were profusely illustrated, and often included custom-made stamps! With each passing year, they became more elaborate, allowing Tolkien to engage, on a smaller scale, in the kind of world building that would make *The Lord of the Rings* so tangible.

Father Christmas is assisted in most of the letters by the bumbling but loveable North Polar Bear, but many other visitors pass in and out of the Secondary World of the North Pole: Snow-elves, Red Gnomes, Snow-men, Cave-bears, and an Elf named Ilbereth.

In the letter from 1933, Father Christmas recounts an attack of Goblins who "have been fearfully wild and angry ever since we took all their stolen toys off them last year and dosed them with green smoke." Though the Red Gnomes chase the Goblins out of their caves, they eventually return, at which point they are decisively beaten by the Polar Bear.

Tolkien includes a picture of the Bear defeating the Goblins, and then comments: "Polar Bear was squeezing, squashing, trampling, boxing and kicking goblins skyhigh, and roaring like a zoo, and the goblins were yelling like engine whistles. He was splendid."

The Adventures of Tom Bombadil

The sixteen poems that make up the collection come, so Tolkien the editor tells us in the Preface, from the same Red Book that contains *The Lord of the Rings*: with some of them appearing on loose leaves and others being scribbled in the margin. The poems he has chosen to include, the editor explains, are "mainly concerned with legends and jests of the Shire at the end of the Third Age, that appear to have been made by Hobbits, especially by Bilbo and his friends, or their immediate descendants."

The poems connect loosely to *The Lord of the Rings* through such characters as Tom Bombadil, the Man in the Moon, Trolls, and an Oliphaunt, though what they really capture is the innocence and yearning for simple joys found in the Shire. The last three poems go a bit deeper and are worth reading alongside the legendarium.

"The Hoard" (#14) connects the dragon from *Beowulf* with the dragon (Smaug) from *The Hobbit*, both of whom are consumed by their stolen treasure of gold and jewels. But the poem goes deeper than that. By telling the sad tale of a priceless hoard fashioned by Noldor-like Elves that passes down, in turn, from a dwarf to a dragon to a human king, Tolkien explores the nature of greed, loneliness, and paranoia that runs throughout *The Silmarillion*, *The Hobbit*, and *The Lord of the Rings*. In the end, all the possessors of the horde are destroyed by their lust for the treasure, and the horde is lost and forgotten.

In "The Sea-Bell" (#15), the first-person speaker goes on a journey into the murky realms of faerie, where he fancies himself a king, spends a year in darkness, and wakes to find he is old and alone. Like Gollum, he becomes a border figure, cut off from all fellowship.

"The Last Ship" (#16) is a poignant, deeply moving poem about the last ship to leave the Grey Havens for Valinor. As they prepare to depart Middle-earth, the elves sing:

> "To mortal fields say farewell,
>   Middle-earth forsaking!
> In Elvenhome a clear bell
>   in the high tower is shaking.
> Here grass fades and leaves fall,
>   and sun and moon wither,
> and we have heard the far call
>   that bids us journey thither."

An Earth-maiden gazes on them from the shore, and they invite her to enter the boat. But she is a mortal woman and cannot join them on their journey. She can only watch as the boat slips away and is gone, ending the time of the Elves in Middle-earth.

Smith of Wootton Major

"Smith of Wootton Major" tells the story of a boy who eats a magic star hidden in a magic cake that becomes a passport allowing him to enter Faerie. For many long years, he journeys in and out of what Tolkien called the perilous realms, even meeting and dancing with the Fairy Queen; but, in the end, he must surrender the star so it may pass on to another chosen child. Unlike Gollum with the Ring, he freely gives up his treasure.

Through his journeys, Smith learns something that Tolkien hoped readers of his epic would learn about the magical lands of Elves: "that the marvels of Faery cannot be approached without danger, and that many of the Evils cannot be challenged without weapons of power too great for any mortal to wield." Tolkien always hated stories that portrayed fairies and elves as small, delicate, and harmless. The realms to which Smith travels fill him with a numinous dread beyond the ken of short-lived mortals:

"He stood beside the Sea of Windless Storm where the blue waves like snow-clad hills roll silently out of Unlight to the long strand, bearing the white ships that return from battles on the Dark Marches of which men know nothing. He saw a great ship cast high upon the land, and the waters fell back in foam without a sound. The elven mariners were tall and terrible; their swords shone and their spears glinted and a piercing light was in their eye. Suddenly they lifted up their voices in a song of triumph, and his heart was shaken with fear, and he fell upon his face, and they passed over him and went away into the echoing hills."

Farmer Giles of Ham

"Farmer Giles of Ham" is a far lighter, less melancholy tale than "Smith of Wootton Major." Rather than reflect Tolkien's fascination with Faerie, it embodies his love of language and wordplay. In brief, it tells the story of how the wily but bourgeois and risk-aversive Farmer Ham defeats a giant, makes a bargain with a dragon, wins a fortune, and gets himself crowned king. Although Tolkien was a believer in rightful hierarchy, he was also a man of the people who respected laborers who lived simple, uncomplicated lives.

Rather than set his tale in Middle-earth, Tolkien the editor sets it in old Britain in the days before King Arthur, a time when "people were richly endowed with names" and "this island was still happily divided into many kingdoms." As in the Shire, the people are independent, live close to the earth, and are settled in their ways. Like Bilbo, they have little desire to see the wide world, preferring to stay in the village they know and love.

For all the crazy and unexpected things that happen in the story, Tolkien states at the outset the kind of slow-paced life he prefers, whether in England or the Shire: "The time was not one of hurry or bustle. But bustle has very little to do with business. Men did their work without it; and they got through a deal both of work and of talk."

Leaf By Niggle

This strange little story is one of the few allegories that Tolkien wrote. It concerns an artist who has tried his whole life to paint a perfect leaf but has been distracted by his neighbors and by life itself. In the tale, he finds himself in purgatory, where he is given the chance to finish the Tree he has dreamed of creating his whole life.

> "Before him stood the Tree, his Tree, finished. If you could say that of a Tree that was alive, its leaves opening, its branches growing and bending in the wind that Niggle had so often felt or guessed, and had

so often failed to catch. He gazed at the Tree, and slowly he lifted his arms and opened them wide.

'It's a gift!' he said. He was referring to his art and also to the result; but he was using the word quite literally."

It's a gift!

For Tolkien, creativity was a gift of God that needed to be used properly. That Niggle's life work should manifest itself as a tree is fitting for an author who loved trees and whose legendarium stretches from the Two Trees to the White Tree of Gondor. It is also fitting, for Tolkien had a tendency to niggle away on details rather than finish his tales.

TWENTY
The Letters of J. R. R. Tolkien

THOUGH I HAVE BORROWED substantially from Tolkien's letters over the course of this book, I will end here by cataloguing some of the letters in which Tolkien mentions details and analyses that I have not yet covered in this book but that shed light on his legendarium. I shall reference the letters by the number which Humphrey Carpenter assigns them in his 1981 edition of *The Letters of J. R. R. Tolkien.*

66: There were Orcs on both sides of WWII who would have used the Ring if they had had it in their possession.

107: Gandalf is an Odin-like wanderer.

109: The only "allegory" behind the Ring is that one cannot fight power with power.

131: In *The Silmarillion*, the sun is *not* a symbol of the divine; it is inferior to the original light of the Two Trees.

131: The true art and poetry of Men can be traced back to the mingling of the blood of Men and Elves that culminates with Aragorn and Arwen.

131: To gain power, Sauron had to let much of himself pass *into* the Ring, an inanimate object. That is why when the Ring is destroyed, Sauron ceases to be.

144: Tom Bombadil is intentionally an enigma. He renounces power and takes a simple delight in all things; yet, it would be bad for him if Sauron won. Tom Bombadil is wrong to think he can be neutral.

144: Elves are like Men but with longer lives and greater beauty, creativity, and nobility.

153: The Númenóreans call on Elbereth as a Roman Catholic might call on a saint.

154: Frodo will not come back from the west, as Arthur will not return from Avalon.

156: Gandalf was sent back from death by Ilúvatar, not by the Valar. Before he came back as Gandalf the White, he could not have exorcised Théoden or defeated Saruman.

156: After Sauron falls, there is no more incarnate Evil; myth gives way to history.

176: Tolkien compares the Dwarves to Jews, resident aliens who have no native land.

180: Tolkien does not know the names and deeds of the other two wizards.

183: We can have moral clarity, but that does not mean people are purely good or evil. There can be a good side in a war, even if individual men on that side do evil things.

191: We can, like Frodo, be put in situations beyond our control that we cannot resist.

192: The logic of the plot demands that Frodo must fail. Still, though the hero fails, the cause does not. Frodo deserves honor for making it so far!

199: When Tolkien wrote "Leaf by Niggle," he feared he would not finish his epic.

211: It is not Tolkien's fault that Ilúvatar did not kill Sauron.

246: Sam is transformed by his loyalty to Frodo. Though noble, he *can* be a bit smug and cocksure with his limited experience and his proverbial wisdom.

281: *The Lord of the Rings* is not about overcoming the bourgeois smugness of the Hobbits, but about the special grace that is given to Bilbo and Frodo.

328: The chosen instruments of God are always imperfect. In *The Lord of the Rings*, the light of truth comes *through* Tolkien, not from him, like light from an invisible lamp.

329: *The Lord of the Rings* is not a novel but a heroic romance.

Annotated Bibliography

Books by Tolkien

At the end of chapter one, I listed all the major books that Tolkien published during his lifetime, along with those edited and published posthumously by his son Christopher. Most of these books are available in numerous editions, and I leave readers to choose which ones best suit their taste. After you read *The Hobbit* and *The Lord of the Rings*, you will want to read *The Silmarillion*, but you might find it helpful to read *The Children of Húrin* first; it is more accessible and will get you used to the strangeness of *The Silmarillion*. If you eventually make it through *The Silmarillion*, do read *Unfinished Tales* and then, if you are still game, *The Book of Lost Tales*, Parts I and II.

I myself would recommend a one-volume edition of *The Lord of the*

Rings, since that is how Tolkien meant his epic to be read. However, it is also nice to curl up with smaller books, and there are many great box sets out there of *The Fellowship of the Ring*, *The Two Towers*, and *The Return of the King*. The ones illustrated by Alan Lee are well worth having. There is also a hardcover edition of *The Silmarillion* with excellent illustrations by Ted Nasmith (Houghton Mifflin, 2004) that bring the epic alive. Do make sure to purchase a version of *The Hobbit* that includes Tolkien's illustrations.

As for the smaller works, I would strongly recommend *A Tolkien Miscellany* (Houghton Mifflin, 2002), which includes under one cover *The Adventures of Tom Bombadil*, "Smith of Wootton Major," "Farmer Giles of Ham," "Leaf By Niggle," "On Fairy-stories," and Tolkien's translations of *Sir Gawain and the Green Knight*, "Pearl," and "Sir Orfeo." Better yet, all of the poetry and fiction is illustrated by Pauline Baynes, who is best known as the original illustrator for The Chronicles of Narnia.

Audio/Video Resources

If you want to experience *The Lord of the Rings* in a memorable way, purchase the thirteen-part BBC radio play version by Brian Sibley (1981). It is excellent and is best listened to with families on long car trips. The unabridged audio book version read by Rob Inglis is a true labor of love and is great for long commutes to work. As I write this, Andy Serkis, who played Gollum in *The Lord of the Rings* films, is narrating his own audio book.

Speaking of that trilogy of films by Peter Jackson, it must be watched over and over again, preferably in the extended edition. (If you purchase the extended edition, make sure to watch the documentaries.) It brings the epic to life in a way that no other fantasy film has ever done. It makes changes, but they are true to the spirit of the novel and render it accessible to the widest possible viewing audience. Peter Jackson followed up with a trilogy of films of *The Hobbit*, which is far less good—not because Jackson lost his touch, but because the novel does not have the depth needed for a three-part film epic!

There is an animated version of *The Hobbit* that was made for TV in 1997 by Rankin-Bass. It is delightful for all ages! In 1978, Ralph Bakshi made an animated version of the first half of the epic. It is odd and uses an odd form of animation, but true fans will want to see this at some point for Bakshi's different interpretations of some of the characters.

There is a four-DVD set called *The J. R. R. Tolkien Audio Collection* that allows listeners to hear Tolkien read the riddle match from *The Hobbit*, the poems and songs from *The Lord of the Rings*, and several poems from *The Adventures of Tom Bombadil*. It also includes his son Christopher reading the tale of Beren and Lúthien from *The Silmarillion*.

Finally, make sure to watch the film *Tolkien* (2019), directed by Dome Karukoski and staring Nicholas Hoult and Lily Collins. It does a beautiful job capturing Tolkien's early friendship with the members of the T.C.B.S. and his love affair with Edith Bratt. It fails to do justice to his Catholic faith, but in all other areas, it offers a faithful depiction.

Biographies and Resource Books

There is still only one authorized biography of J. R. R. Tolkien: Humphrey Carpenter's *Tolkien* (Allen & Unwin, 1977). It is very good and is the best place to start your acquaintance with Tolkien the man. Carpenter also selected and edited *The Letters of J. R. R. Tolkien* (Allen & Unwin, 1981), which is a must-read. Finally his *The Inklings: C. S. Lewis, J. R. R. Tolkien, Charles Williams, and Their Friends* (Houghton Mifflin, 1979) offers a group biography of the main members of the Inklings.

For more on Tolkien's faith and its impact on his life, see Joseph Pearce's *Tolkien: Man and Myth* (Ignatius Press, 1998). For the influences in Tolkien's life and reading that impacted his work, see T. A. Shippey's *The Road to Middle-Earth* (Houghton Mifflin, 1982) and Holly Ordway's *Tolkien's Modern Reading* (Word on Fire, 2021). The latter book fairly critiques the shortcomings of Carpenter's biography.

For more on the friendship between Tolkien and Lewis and how it affected their work, see Diana Glyer's *The Company They Keep: C. S. Lewis and J. R. R. Tolkien as Writers in Community* (Kent State UP, 2008) and Colin Duriez's *Tolkien and the Lord of the Rings: A Guide to Middle-Earth* (HiddenSpring, 2001). For the life-long effect that the T.C.B.S. and WWI had on Tolkien, I would strongly recommend John Garth's *Tolkien and the Great War* (Houghton Mifflin, 2013).

Two resources that every Tolkien fan must have on his shelf are Karen Wynn Fonstad's *The Atlas of Middle-Earth* (Houghton Mifflin, 1991) and Robert Foster's *The Complete Guide to Middle-Earth: Tolkien's World from A to Z* (Ballantine, 1974). I would also recommend Wayne G. Hammond and Christopher Scull's *J. R. R. Tolkien: Artist & Illustrator* (Houghton Mifflin, 2000). I have learned a great deal about Tolkien's literary influences by working my way through *The Tolkien Fan's Medieval Reader* (Cold Spring Press, 2004), whose editor, David E. Smith, identifies himself by the pseudonym Turgon of TheOneRing.net.

Books about Tolkien

Two general studies that map out the web of influences of Tolkien's Christian faith on his theology and philosophy are Ralph Wood's *The Gospel According to Tolkien: Visions of the Kingdom in Middle-earth* (Westminster John Knox, 2003) and Peter Kreeft's *The Philosophy of Tolkien: The Worldview Behind The Lord of the Rings* (Ignatius, 2005).

For narrower, more focused studies of the influence of his faith, see Bradley Birzer's *J. R. R. Tolkien's Sanctifying Myth: Understanding Middle-Earth* (ISI Books, 2002), Stratford Caldecott's *Secret Fire: The Spiritual Vision of J. R. R. Tolkien* (Darton, Longman, and Todd, 2003), and Rutledge Fleming's *The Battle for Middle-earth: Tolkien's Divine Design in The Lord of the Rings* (Eerdmans, 2004). C. R. Wiley's brief but delightful *In the House of Tom Bombadil* (Canon Press, 2021) offers excellent insight into why Tolkien included Bombadil and Goldberry in his epic fantasy.

Jonathan Witt and J. W. Richards's *The Hobbit Party: The Vision of Freedom That Tolkien Got and the West Forgot* (Ignatius, 2014) explores the social, political, and economic dimensions of Tolkien's Shire. Michael

Jahosky's *The Good News of the Return of the King: The Gospel in Middle-Earth* (Wipf & Stock, 2020) offers a fresh reading of Tolkien's epic as a parable writ large. Philip Ryken's *The Messiah Comes to Middle-Earth: Images of Christ's Threefold Office in the Lord of the Rings* (IVP, 2017) sheds light on Gandalf the prophet, Aragorn the king, and Frodo (and Sam) the priest.

For three difficult but original and rewarding studies, see Joshua Hren's *Middle-earth and the Return of the Common Good: J. R. R. Tolkien and Political Philosophy* (Cascade Books, 2018), Lisa Coutras's *Tolkien's Theology of Beauty: Majesty, Splendor, and Transcendence in Middle-earth* (Palgrave Macmillan, 2016), and Jonathan S. McIntosh's *The Flame Imperishable: Tolkien, St. Thomas, and the Metaphysics of Faërie* (Angelico Press, 2017).

In my *On the Shoulders of Hobbits: The Road to Virtue with Tolkien and Lewis* (Moody, 2012), I survey how *The Lord of the Rings* and The Chronicles of Narnia embody the seven classical and theological virtues, wrestle with the nature of friendship and of evil, and explore what it means to be pilgrims in a good but fallen world. In my *From A to Z to Middle-earth with J. R. R. Tolkien* (Lampion Press, 2016), I offer an overview of the main themes in Tolkien's legendarium and complete reviews of the Peter Jackson films.

About the Author

LOUIS MARKOS (https://www.amazon.com/author/louismarkos) holds a BA in English and History from Colgate University and an MA and PhD in English from the University of Michigan.

He is a Professor of English and Scholar in Residence at Houston Baptist University, where he holds the Robert H. Ray Chair in Humanities. He teaches courses on British Romantic and Victorian Poetry and Prose, the Classics, C. S. Lewis and J. R. R. Tolkien, and Film.

He is the author of twenty-four published books and two lecture series with the Teaching Company/Great Courses (The Life and Writings of C. S. Lewis; Plato to Postmodernism: Understanding the Essence of Literature and the Role of the Author).

He has published 300 articles and reviews in such journals as Christianity Today, Touchstone, Theology Today, Christian Research Journal, Mythlore, Christian Scholar's Review, Saint Austin Review,

American Arts Quarterly, and The City, and had his modern adaptation of Euripides' Iphigenia in Tauris, Euripides' Helen, and Sophocles' Electra performed off-Broadway.

He is a popular speaker in Houston, and has given over 300 public lectures on such topics as C. S. Lewis, apologetics, education, ancient Greece, ancient Rome, and Dante in over two dozen states and in British Columbia, Canada, Oxford, England, and Rome.

He is committed to the concept of the Professor as Public Educator and believes that knowledge must not be walled up in the Academy but must be disseminated to all who have ears to hear.

About the Illustrator

JEFF FALLOW has been illustrating For Beginners books since 1999.

Previous books include *Stanislavski For Beginners* by David Allen, *London For Beginners* by Nita Clarke, and more recently *First Amendment For Beginners* by Michael J. LaMonica. Jeff has worked as illustrator for Glasgow Museums and graphic designer for the National Health Service. He is Scottish and lives in the Kingdom of Fife, an ancient part of Scotland and the home of golf (which he doesn't play).

His hobbies include taxidermy (using roadkill) and making steampunk creations (using overkill).

THE FOR BEGINNERS® SERIES

THE FOR BEGINNERS® SERIES

THE FOR BEGINNERS® SERIES